Ponymagic

Animal Magic

Have you read them all?

Look out for more books by
HOLLY WEBB

and the Enchanted Door

www.holly-webb.com

Animal Magic

Ponymagic

HOLLY WEBB

Scholastic Children's Books
An imprint of Scholastic Ltd
Euston House, 24 Eversholt Street
London, NW1 1DB, UK
Registered office: Westfield Road, Southam, Warwickshire, CV47 0RA
SCHOLASTIC and associated logos are trademarks and/or
registered trademarks of Scholastic Inc.

First published in the UK by Scholastic Ltd, 2010
This edition published by Scholastic Ltd, 2013

ISBN 978 1 407 13557 1

A CIP catalogue record for this book is available
from the British Library.

Printed and bound by CPI Group (UK) Ltd, Croydon, CR0 4YY
Papers used by Scholastic Children's Books are made from
wood grown in sustainable forests.

For Jon, Tom, Robin and William

Chapter 1

Lottie smiled and turned over in her sleep, stretching her toes down to the end of the bed. Beside her, her dachshund, Sofie, growled to herself and shook her ears, dreaming of hunting something small and delicious. A cake, perhaps.

Lottie slept on quietly, but her mind went travelling, far away from Grace's Pet Shop, the magical place where she had lived for the last few months and discovered she had magical powers of her own. Shrugging her duvet away from her shoulders, Lottie peered excitedly between the dark trees. It was sunrise in her dream. The chill of the night was fading and soft golden light was starting to filter through the upper canopy of a rainforest, stirring the purplish mists that floated around her feet. A bee buzzed by, striped in black and gold, weaving drunkenly from flower to flower as the petals slowly opened in the warmth. Noises grew louder and louder and suddenly a troop of monkeys flung themselves past Lottie, swinging through the branches, leaping and hanging from the looped vines, and shrieking with glee.

Lottie shook out her golden mane, whinnying with surprise, and felt the heady amber and cinnamon scent of her unicorn hair perfume the dawn air.

Sofie sneezed. "Too strong," she muttered, shuddering all over. "Much too strong."

Lottie lowered her head to nudge Sofie gently. "I'm glad you've come too." Lottie had had a dream like this before, where she had been a unicorn. It was when she had first seen the silver unicorn – a unicorn who she had later realized was her own father, under a spell that made him forget who he was. Her father was back with her at the pet shop now, but he

2

had been away for eight whole years, and Lottie was having to learn to love him all over again. It seemed strange that she was closer to a dog than to her own father, but Sofie wasn't just a pet. She was Lottie's familiar – she didn't only talk, she had strong magical powers of her own. Together they could do the most amazing things.

Sofie looked around consideringly. "It is very *green*."

Lottie shook her head, her mane flinging out in another waft of scent. "When I saw my dad before, it was a wintry place with a lake. I'm sure of it. Climb on my back, Sofie, you'll see when you're higher up. This must be the rainforest. Where the real unicorns are."

Sofie eyed her suspiciously. "Are you saying I am not tall enough like I am, Lottie?" As a dachshund, she could be touchy about her short legs although she was very graceful.

Lottie whickered in amusement. "No, only that it might help you to see what I mean."

Sofie gave a resentful sniff, but she bounded on to a fallen tree covered in emerald moss, and then scrambled up a branch and on to Lottie's caramel-coloured back. Lottie felt her sharp little claws scrabbling and stood still.

Sofie was silent for a moment. "Yes. It is the rainforest, now. Before, when you dreamed the unicorns, it was only a shadow place. There was one black tree, over and over. You would not have seen, Lottie, you do not have the sense for these things that we dogs do. Now this is a true place."

"It has to be because Dad has got his memories back again," Lottie mused, starting to pace forward very gently, so that Sofie did not fall off. "We're inside his memories, after all. I suppose he's unlocked all of this inside his head, so now we can see it too. I wonder if we could come here together? That would be brilliant. I'll have to ask him when we get back. Hey!" She raised her head sharply, sniffing the air, and making Sofie yip with annoyance as she started to slide. Sofie dug her claws in, and Lottie gasped. "Sorry! I forgot you were there for a minute. Sofie, I can smell another unicorn, can't you?"

"I cannot smell anything, with this rose and spices smell in my nose from you all the time," Sofie muttered. But she snuffed loudly. "Mint. Something disgusting under a bush that I do not want to think about. Chocolate. Although I may just be wishing that – ah! *Oui*. More cinnamon. Cinnamon and mint. Yes, Lottie, it is another of these *large* things. A unicorn." She half-slid, half-jumped from Lottie's back, and scrambled up another fallen tree, pointing with her nose like a hunting dog. "He is over there. By the water."

"Is it my dad? Is it a silver unicorn?" Lottie asked, her voice rising in excitement. She had galloped with her father through those trees, which had seemed real to her, even if Sofie didn't think so. It had been one of the most exciting things she had ever done. Lottie shook her mane eagerly, wanting to run, to race, to stretch out the muscles she could feel bunching in her legs.

Sofie rolled her eyes. "I am very clever, Lottie, and my nose is most excellent. But I do not smell in colour. He is bigger than you, and a he, and he has been running. Is that not enough for you?"

"It might be Dad," Lottie murmured, walking softly through the ferns. But there was no glint of a silver unicorn as they paced towards the river. The water was flowing fast and Lottie was sure they were near the waterfall she had seen before. It rattled and chuckled over the stones, making little pools and fast-pouring streamlets, and she longed to wade in it, to feel its icy chill lapping over her hooves, soaking the feathery golden tangles of her fetlocks.

"Look!" Sofie whispered, calling Lottie back as she pawed gently at the bank. "There he is!"

It wasn't her father. Instead of his glorious silver coat, shining like the moon to Lottie's sun, this creature was midnight black. He was stooping to drink, his powerful neck bent, and his mane trailing down towards the water.

Lottie wanted to call him, but she didn't dare. She had never seen a real unicorn, only her father in these strange dreams, but she imagined they would be cautious creatures, living so hidden away.

But some sense of danger must have warned the black unicorn. He swung his head up suddenly and wheeled around, his hind legs splashing into the river. He stared directly at Lottie for a short second; then he leaped into the shallow water, and galloped away, kicking up great clouds of spray that hung in the air and glittered like diamonds.

Lottie sighed, and Sofie yapped crossly after him, but he vanished round the bend of the stream, and they were left staring at the swirling water.

"I didn't even do anything," Lottie muttered. "How could he be frightened of us? I'm a unicorn too!" She glanced down at her golden coat, and the flowing golden mane falling over her shoulders. Then she looked at Sofie, blatantly a small black dachshund with big ginger eyebrows, and not the sort of creature often found in a rainforest. The little dog glared back.

"It is not my fault, Lottie!" she snapped. "I found him for you, did I not?"

"Yes, sorry. . ." Lottie shook her head, and the forest shimmered and melted around her, leaving her blinking in the darkness of her own bedroom.

The next day was Sunday, so Lottie and Sofie slept late. Lottie still felt woozy when she staggered downstairs at about ten. Her dad, Tom, was eating toast in the kitchen and chatting to Horace, the pygmy owl, who was sitting on the teapot like some absurd sort of tea cosy. Her cousin, Danny, had gone to play football, and dragged Uncle Jack with him to watch, which meant Uncle Jack would spend the rest of the day wrapped in scarves and complaining how cold he was.

Horace had been a parrot when Lottie had first met him, and she had thought that was all he was, until her father had come home and explained he was a firebird – a phoenix. Horace could take any shape he liked, though he'd been a parrot for years, ever since Lottie's father had disappeared. Horace had transformed into an enormous owl when Lottie's dad came back, though, and he'd terrified all the mice in the shop. They still didn't like him much as a pygmy owl, but at least in his new form he was keener on beetles for breakfast instead of mice, and they weren't forced to keep having memorial services for Horace's dinner. There was a scaly-looking leg trailing out of Horace's beak now, and Lottie shuddered.

Horace clacked his beak at her and swallowed the leg with an enormous gulp.

"When are you going to *grow*?" Sofie asked him pointedly, nudging Lottie's father to butter her a piece of toast. She had already stared at Lottie until she put the kettle on and got the coffee tin out.

Horace ruffled up all his feathers haughtily. "I don't know, cheeky little madam. It was a very strong bit of magic. Believe me, I'm recovering as fast as I can. I very much enjoyed being bigger than you-ou-ou." He hooted the last word expressively, and Sofie recoiled. Horace could still be quite frightening, even when he was a fluffy little ball of feathers.

Lottie thought he was gorgeous as a pygmy owl, and wished he'd stay that way. He was only tiny because he'd used up so much of his strength fighting Pandora – the strange, crazed enchantress who'd destroyed Lottie's father's memory and left him lost and bewildered in the rainforest for eight years. Pandora had known Tom wasn't dead, like everyone believed, but she'd never thought he would return. She had been furious when she found out he was back and had tried to get rid of him properly. She might have managed it, if it hadn't been for Horace. He had flown into Pandora's spell when she went to attack Lottie and her father, and for a while they had thought he was gone for ever.

But it was Pandora who was gone now. Lottie's father could have killed her, and almost had, right here in the shop, when she'd attacked Lottie. Lottie was grateful that he hadn't – she didn't want her father to be someone who could do something as awful as that. But she kept waking up in the middle of the night now, wondering if it had been a mistake.

Pandora had left, but she might come back. And even if she stayed away, she was sneaky enough to work her horrible magic from a distance. She'd sent her memory spells with someone else when she had first attacked Lottie's dad.

Lottie set a large bowl of coffee down in front of Sofie and sat opposite her dad, smiling at him. Just seeing him made her feel happy – he'd been gone for so long. He looked funny now, though, windblown and red-cheeked. He liked to go out walking on Netherbridge Hill before everyone else was up.

"Dad," Lottie asked thoughtfully. "How did Pandora make you lose your memory?"

Her dad sighed. "I'm honestly not sure what the spell was. It was only a short while after I found the unicorns. I was still enthralled by them – I'd even spoken to one of them. It was like a dream. I suppose that's how she got to me. There was a net, I remember that much. A silken net, and after it fell on us, I didn't know who I was – or what I was."

"Us?" Lottie asked, staring at him. "Not just you?"

"No, I was with one of the unicorns," her father explained. "The most beautiful, I thought. He was all black, with the most wonderful shining midnight coat."

Lottie sat bolt upright. "I've seen him! He was in my dream!"

Her father smiled delightedly. "Did he speak to you?" he asked, clearly thrilled.

Lottie shook her head slowly. "No. I didn't know that he could. I suppose they would, though, wouldn't they. . ."

"They are great charmers. . ." Her father smiled, remembering. Then he sighed. "I loved living with them. Even after Pandora's spell, when I didn't know anything any more, and I was only living half a life, I knew that I loved them. They were so beautiful. But Midnight disappeared. He was caught in the net too, you see. He didn't know who he was, either." He rubbed the heels of his hands into his eyes, and swallowed. "He probably still doesn't. . ."

"What happened to him?" Lottie breathed in horror.

"He hid in the deeper parts of the forest. The other unicorns would catch a glimpse of him every so often, but he never spoke any more."

"That's so sad," Lottie whispered.

Her father nodded. "If only I could go back. . . But I can't, Lottie, or I would, to try and save him, now I have my magic back."

"Why can you not go back?" Sofie asked with interest, licking coffee off her whiskery jaws.

"I don't think I could ever find them again," Lottie's dad admitted. "It was half by chance the first time, and then the spell. . . That whole time is almost like a dream now, the most amazing dream – the kind where you wake up and most desperately want it to be real."

Lottie blinked. "But . . . it was real?" she asked, almost pleading. "They are real?"

Her father leaned across the table and hugged her. "Yes, Lottie. I know they are. When I came back here at first, I still wasn't sure whether it had all been a dream. It seemed so strange, remembering only these dreamlike creatures. But I suppose they were my strongest memory, because I'd lived with them after the spell stole my mind." He smiled at her. "And you and your mother were the hardest things to remember, because Pandora wanted to take away the things I loved the most."

Lottie smiled back, but her eyes grew sad, as she thought of the black unicorn, hiding all alone in the forest.

"They are the most amazing creatures," her father said, sipping his tea and staring dreamily into space. "So beautiful – well, you've seen them, Lottie, you know." He grinned at her. "You were a particularly lovely unicorn yourself, Lottie." Then his eyes hardened as he added, "It's probably a good thing that Pandora didn't know you existed when she cast the memory spell. She had no idea of the power we shared."

"She doesn't understand family," Horace put in, his strange, squeaking, squawking voice making Lottie jump. "She never understood how much you and Jack meant to each other, Tom. How important it was that you were brothers. She thought she could drag you apart, and you'd never complain. Huh."

"Doesn't she have a family of her own?" Lottie asked, and her father shook his head.

"Nope. She was an orphan. Her parents both died in an accident when she was very young. Pandora got passed round all sorts of relatives and ended up in Netherbridge when she was about fifteen."

"That sounds really grim," Lottie muttered. She didn't want to feel sorry for Pandora. She *hated* Pandora. But she couldn't help it.

Her father was smiling at her lovingly, but Sofie butted her head into Lottie's arm.

16

"Lottie, you are too soft. She has tried to make you her slave and you are sad because she had an unhappy childhood? Pah!" Sofie glared at her. "I think we should have got rid of her for ever when we had the chance," she spat crossly.

Sofie was so small and sweet-looking that such angry words seemed even worse when she said them, and Lottie gazed at her in despair. Sofie made a funny little huffing noise and hunched her shoulders, as though she were a little ashamed of herself, but she would never admit it. She went back to drinking her coffee, very carefully not looking at Lottie.

"What would have happened to you if Mum hadn't got that job in France?" Lottie wondered aloud, staring wide-eyed at her father. "If it really was me finding my magic that sent the unicorn to you—"

"It was," her father put in firmly. "You know it was. You came to me, and you started to break the spell. Like Horace said, Pandora didn't understand family. It was probably the

17

only way it could be broken – someone with a magical bond to me that was even stronger than the spell."

"Your own magic," Horace pointed out. "Lottie inherited it from you. So you knew it, even enchanted as you were. It was familiar, it called to you." He buried his beak in his fluffy chest feathers for a moment. "I should have gone after you," he hooted mournfully. "All those years. . . I could have transformed into something seagoing. An albatross. I should have made the journey. But we were so sure you would come back, and then the weeks stretched so quickly into months. . . And the trail was cold, and I had no energy left for transformation. The whole place was lifeless without you." He hooted dolefully. "It took a child to chase you out. A child!"

"My child, Horace." Lottie's father smiled. "That makes it very different, as you said." Then he shivered, staring at Lottie. "I don't know what would have happened if you hadn't found me, Lottie. I would have stayed, I suppose. I didn't realize how much time I was spending as a unicorn anyway; perhaps I would have transformed for good, and stayed there for ever." He grinned. "It would have its advantages. It really would have been for ever, for a start. Unicorns are immortal, you know."

Lottie was staring at him with her mouth open. "Transformed? What, you mean, you actually *were* a unicorn? Not just looking like a unicorn in those weird visions I had?"

"It's a secret, hidden valley, Lottie," her dad explained. "A place of magic and enchantment. It stays that way. So, it's only protection. You find it, and you stay long enough – you start to change. It takes a long time. I mean, I was there a good many years and I wasn't completely transformed, just flicking from one form to another – human to unicorn. But if I'd stayed much longer, I would have been a unicorn for ever. There were a couple of others in the herd who'd been humans who had found the valley."

Sofie leaned forward, staring at him very seriously. Tom looked back at her with an anxious frown, unsure what she was going to say. Sofie fixed him with a sharp stare, and whispered, "I must ask you this. Did you eat grass?" She shuddered at the thought, still gazing at him.

Lottie and her dad spluttered with laughter, and Horace gave a squawk of disgust at Sofie's silliness.

Sofie looked around the table in what seemed like honest bewilderment. "What? It is a very important question! Grass, ugh. I cannot think of it."

"It was the best grass, Sofie." Lottie's dad chuckled. "Really tasty. Always fresh; there was one little patch in a clearing, you'd swear it tasted like . . . oh, like chocolate."

Sofie nodded. "Hmm. I do not believe that is so, but perhaps. A pity you did not bring any back. Lottie eats far too much chocolate. A grass version might be better for her."

Lottie laughed out loud. "You eat more than me and I'm about six times bigger than you!"

"Exactly," Sofie told her wisely. "And I do not get pimples, either, Lottie, *ma belle*."

"You will have to go back." Horace's voice was quiet, but it broke through the laughter sharply.

"But I can't," Lottie's dad looked at his hands, as though he didn't want to say this with Lottie and Horace watching. "I would go if I could – though I promise I would come back, Lottie, I swear to you. But really, I don't know where to go." He shook his head wearily. "That part of my mind, it's still foggy. Confused. I can't remember the journey back; I was still half-enchanted."

Horace's huge eyes shone yellow against his silvery feathers. "You will. I know. You will all go back."

Lottie shivered. It sounded like a prophecy, as though Horace *knew*. Could phoenixes foretell the future? He had never mentioned it, though of course he'd never mentioned being a phoenix either, so who knew.

Then Horace blinked slowly, and peered shyly at Lottie's dad's plate. "Is that Marmite on those toast crusts?" he asked in a hopeful sort of way. "I need to build up my strength."

Chapter 2

A grey November Monday in Netherbridge seemed a long way away from the Indian rainforests. Lottie hurried to meet her best friend, Ruby, at the bridge, feeling rather disappointed that it was only boring old English mist, not rainforest humidity she was walking through.

"I'm really not looking forward to this morning," Ruby muttered grumpily as Lottie joined her on the bridge. "Assembly's torture anyway, without having to be in charge of it."

Lottie stopped in the middle of the pavement, causing a woman with a pushchair to run into her feet. Luckily the baby thought it was very funny, so the mother just sighed at her irritably.

"You'd forgotten?" Ruby asked her in disbelief. "OK, what happened to you this weekend then, because we spent the whole of last week moaning about it."

Lottie grinned. "I'm quite glad I forgot. Sorry. I was talking to my dad about what really happened when he was away. Somehow it never seemed like the right time to ask him before."

Ruby sighed. "I could get kidnapped, or run away to join the circus, and I'd still never manage to have a more exciting weekend than you. It isn't fair." But she was smiling. "So, was it OK? I mean, you're not upset about what he told you?"

Lottie looked thoughtfully at her feet as they walked along. "No. I don't think so. I mean, it's really weird, thinking about him being so far away, but it helps to know what happened. Not that he can remember a lot of it, not properly."

"I don't suppose you could knock up a quick memory loss spell for me after this morning, could you?" Ruby said hopefully. "I don't want to remember being a dancing Dalmatian, it's too cruel. Or even better, have you got anything that would make me throw up? Then I wouldn't have to do it at all."

Lottie giggled. "Have you got your ears?" she asked, and Ruby scowled.

"Unfortunately, yes. Mrs Taylor would just have made me ring my mum to bring them if I'd said I'd forgotten."

Lottie and Ruby's class were organizing school assembly in aid of a charity that morning, and the class had voted to support the local animal shelter, which was in Sandford, the next town. Lottie loved the idea of helping the animal shelter, but her class had to organize everything themselves, and hateful Zara Martin and her gang of friends had taken the job over.

Zara couldn't stand Ruby, who'd hated her back ever since they started infants' school together six years before, and Zara absolutely hated Lottie. She'd bullied Lottie ever since she had arrived in Netherbridge. Lottie had ended up accidentally casting a spell to make their class see what Zara was really like, showing all her horrible little ways so for once everyone saw the pure nastiness at her heart. Lottie had to make them forget the magic of it all afterwards, but no one had ever looked at Zara quite the same way again.

Mrs Taylor still thought of her as a perfect pupil, though, and had been very glad to hand over the organization of assembly to someone so keen. She hadn't understood that what Zara was so keen on was embarrassing everyone she didn't like. As a result, most of the girls in Lottie and Ruby's class were being dancing puppies. Luckily for Lottie, Mrs Taylor had decided she had a loud speaking voice, and had hauled her out of the dance – where she would have been a bulldog, as Zara's official least favourite person – and given her loads of stuff about the shelter to read out.

Thankfully, after a panicked search, Lottie found that her speech was still in her bag, where she had put it on Friday and ignored it for the whole weekend. "That's OK then. I was sure I'd lost it." Lottie sighed. "I wish Ariadne hadn't said in my last magic lesson that magic shouldn't be used except for the best of reasons. I would so like to magic up some smoke under the sprinklers just before assembly. This is going to be a nightmare."

"Excuse me," Ruby pointed out frostily. "Are you wearing a costume? No. So you have nothing to complain about."

Lottie grinned. "Ah, but you look so cute in those spotty ears," she told Ruby, giggling, and she dodged away as Ruby swung her school bag menacingly.

Most of Lottie and Ruby's class were standing around in a sulky huddle when they got into the playground. Even those who weren't being forced to dance had to hold up posters, and everyone had to sing an unbelievably awful song that Zara had made up. Lottie's sprinkler idea would be very popular, if only she could really make it work.

"Someone would think we had set off a real fire, and we'd get in loads of trouble," she admitted regretfully to Ruby. It seemed to be a situation where magical abilities were no use. Lottie stared resentfully at Zara, who was bossing around all the girls in the dance. Lily looked like she was almost crying.

"Ignore her," Ruby leaned over to tell Lily, as Zara went to find someone else to bully. "It isn't you doing it wrong, it's just a really stupid dance."

"I get it wrong every time she looks at me," Lily muttered miserably.

"It probably looks better wrong," Lottie reassured her. "She's a useless choreographer."

"Why did Mrs Taylor let her take it all over?" Lily complained, and Ruby and Lottie exchanged glances. A few weeks ago, no one in the class would have asked that. Lottie wasn't sure what it was about Zara that gave her such a hold over everyone at school, but it was definitely fading. Lily was glaring after Zara furiously now. "She's so horrible," she whispered to Ruby and Lottie, her eyes wide, as though it was something she'd only just realized.

"Um, yeah!" Ruby agreed.

"I used to really like her," Lily said, her voice thoughtful. "But . . . she's always been mean. Hasn't she?" She sighed. "The thing is, I'm still scared of her, even if I don't like her any more. But I don't care if she likes me or not," she added, sounding almost amazed.

"Me neither. But we still have to be dancing dogs," Ruby pointed out gloomily.

That morning's assembly had the same amazing powers as a spelling test – it actually made school go faster, when usually it dragged out second by second. Now it seemed as though registration had lasted seconds, and they were lining up on the stage behind the big curtains, listening to the rest of the school walking in and the teachers telling everyone to be quiet.

Lottie swallowed hard. She was standing by the edge of the stage, holding the script she had to read from after the dance. She wished desperately that she hadn't enjoyed the book they'd been reading in class so much – if she hadn't liked it, she wouldn't have read so well and Mrs Taylor wouldn't have chosen her to do this. She felt sick at the thought of the whole school watching her. She'd been in school plays before, and dance shows, but then she'd been playing a part and that had made it easier somehow. She'd never felt as awful as this before. Her head was spinning, and she was seriously beginning to think she might faint. *I mustn't*, she murmured to herself. It would be so embarrassing. Even more embarrassing than a bulldog outfit.

Mrs Taylor beamed round at everybody and whispered, "Enjoy yourselves!" as though she was giving them all an enormous treat, and started to open the curtains.

Lottie hardly saw the dance. She didn't notice when the dancing Dalmatian *accidentally* went the wrong way and barged straight into Zara, who was wearing her sparkly silver leotard and dancing the starring role. No one was quite sure what she was meant to be, even Mrs Taylor, but it hadn't stopped her. Zara fell over and the whole school held its breath for the merest second, and then sniggered, rather nastily.

Except for Lottie, who was staring at her script and wishing that the words would stop swimming across the page.

When the dance finally ended, with all the dogs posed round Zara, scowling, except for the Dalmatian who looked remarkably satisfied with itself, Lottie was supposed to step forward and explain what they were raising money for.

Her feet didn't want to move. Lottie tried to focus on them, to make them move, but her brain didn't seem to be connected to the rest of her body any more. Nothing happened. Vaguely, Lottie wondered when all those trees had grown at the back of the school hall. She didn't remember them from PE on Friday.

Everyone was staring at her now, but Lottie hardly noticed. The faces of the other children were fading out and she couldn't hear Mrs Taylor prompting her, more and more irritably. Lottie wasn't in the crowded school hall any longer. She was somewhere green and humid and full of the sounds of water.

Mrs Taylor and Ruby half-carried her off the stage and Zara announced that Lottie was obviously having a panic attack so they would repeat their dance, as after all, the show must go on.

Lottie didn't hear Zara's gloating voice. She simply walked away from everyone and into the rainforest. She could hear the river, but this time she wasn't going that way. She walked slowly, purposefully, through the trees. She had no idea where she was going, or why, but she had to go on. She knew she must.

She should be able to hear other noises now, now that she was heading away from the rippling of the river, but it was eerily quiet. No bird calls, which seemed strange. No monkeys shrieking, as there had been before. *Maybe I'm scaring them away*, Lottie wondered. She was herself this time, wearing a red school cardigan that was much too hot. It was unlikely that the creatures in this forest had seen a human since her father had left. Probably everything was hiding. Lottie looked around rather sadly and suddenly wished that Sofie could be there again too.

Why wasn't she? Lottie frowned. Surely Sofie should be with her. Her mind felt strangely empty without the comforting presence of her familiar. Even when Sofie was asleep, usually Lottie could sense her, curled up somewhere in her thoughts.

A horse's angry cry suddenly jolted Lottie out of her worried mind-search and she realized that hoofbeats were thudding over the forest floor, and getting closer. Instinctively, she drew back against the trunk of a huge tree, trying to work out where the noise was coming from, but it seemed to be hammering and shaking all around her. Lottie pressed her hands back against the mossy bark of the tree, feeling as though those hoofbeats might shake her loose and send her flying somewhere strange and wild.

Thundering towards her, weaving dangerously through the trees, came the black unicorn she had seen in her dream. His head was down, and his hooves were beating the ground in a mesmerizing rhythm. He seemed to be able to place his feet without worrying about the fallen branches, but just before he reached Lottie there was a massive, half-rotten tree trunk. Lottie watched him coming towards her, thinking that surely he would have to swerve around it, and then hopefully he would veer away past her, never seeing her, and she could somehow find her way home. . .

But he didn't swerve. He jumped. A huge, soaring leap, his legs drawn up under him like a champion showjumper. He jumped, staring into Lottie's eyes with his black ones, and he landed right in front of her, so close that she could feel his breath on her face as he stood there, his sides heaving from his gallop. The horn on his forehead was polished black, and lethally, cruelly sharp.

Lottie looked up at him, her heart thudding, sure she could almost hear his thumping in time. When she had seen him with Sofie, she had wanted to run after him, meet him, stroke him. Now he was close enough for her to touch and she was terrified.

Help me, he whispered in her head.

Lottie stared. It was the last thing she had expected him to say, because she had been thinking that the black unicorn was chasing her, that his desperate gallop had been after her.

But it hadn't been. He had been running from something else. Something that was now chasing them both. Hunting them down.

Lottie could hear it striding, swishing, coming after them, and she did the only thing she could think to do. She put her arms around the black unicorn's neck and held him tight, pouring all her power and magic into him and turning them to fight.

Lottie woke gasping, fighting to sit up. Why was she lying down? What had happened? She blinked, her vision adapting slowly to the strange lack of trees.

She was at school. Someone was holding her. Lottie turned slowly, still unsure what was going on and half-expecting to find an enormous black horse next to her. But it was Ruby, still wearing an absurd black and white furry headband with ears stuck on to it. It looked particularly wrong round her white and worried face.

"Lottie, what happened?" she whispered. "Mrs Taylor thinks you just got nervous, and I thought you probably wouldn't want anyone asking questions, so I told her you were really worried about this morning and you'd said you hadn't had any breakfast. So hopefully she'll just write it down that you fainted. She's gone to the office to phone your uncle."

"Great," Lottie muttered. "Fainting on stage. Zara's going to love that."

"Sorry. . ." Ruby looked really upset, and Lottie struggled to sit up so she could see her properly. She was in the medical room, she realized, lying on a very uncomfortable bed.

"Hey, I didn't mean it like that. Oh. . ." Lottie's head swam, and she leaned back against the wall feeling dizzy and sick.

"Don't go again!" Ruby gasped, and she sounded so frightened that Lottie opened her eyes at once and stared at her.

"I just felt dizzy," she promised, looking worriedly at her friend. "Ruby, why are you so upset?" She sat up again, more carefully this time. "And how come you had to lie to Mrs Taylor that it was just nerves and I fainted because I hadn't eaten?" Lottie eyed Ruby grimly. "It could have been true and then you'd just be telling me what an idiot I was. What did I do, Ruby?"

"Nothing," Ruby muttered, and then she shook her head when Lottie scowled at her. "Really! Nothing. You just stood there. But it was scary, Lottie. You were there, but you weren't. Your eyes were just like glass and there was nothing behind them. It looked. . ." She shrugged, embarrassed. "Spooky. Sorry. . ."

Lottie swallowed. Ruby had never been scared of her and her powers before. Until now, Ruby had only seen the fun side of magic – like the gorgeous talking animals in the shop. Pandora had bewitched Ruby a few weeks before, hoping to trap Lottie. Ruby had been under the spell for days, but she hadn't really known anything about it, so she'd never had time to be scared.

"Did I say anything?" Lottie asked slowly.

Ruby nodded, but she didn't seem to want to look at Lottie.

"Ruby, you have to tell me!" Lottie thought she could remember what had happened in the rainforest, but it was patchy and confused. She wanted to know everything.

"What happened?" Ruby asked again in a whisper. "Please, Lottie, I was so scared. What were you doing?"

Lottie sighed. "Being chased by a unicorn. Or I thought I was. Then it turned out something else was chasing us both. He wanted me to rescue him."

"Oh..." Ruby blinked. "I guess that explains why you screamed then."

"In front of everyone?" Lottie asked, feeling

sick again.

Ruby shook her head. "No, out in the corridor, when me and Mrs Taylor were bringing you here. You sounded awful."

"It was probably when I thought this enormous black unicorn was about to jump on top of me," Lottie muttered. "I didn't mean to drag you into all this," she told Ruby, pleating the horrible paper sheet on the bed between her fingers.

"I don't mind being dragged in." Ruby sat close beside her, staring at the sheet and adding a pattern of holes round Lottie's pleats. "It was scary because it didn't look like you. When you put that spell on Zara you didn't look like that. I didn't know if you were OK."

Lottie nodded. "I've never seen anyone else do what I did. I'd probably freak too."

"Was it a vision?" Ruby asked hesitantly.

"I suppose . . . I don't know what it's called. I've never just had one in the middle of the day like that. Usually I dream them." Lottie frowned worriedly. "It had better not start happening all the time, everyone'll think I'm crazy!"

Ruby said nothing, and Lottie looked at her. She was still gazing at the paper, stabbing holes in it with her nails.

"They think I'm crazy already, don't they?" Lottie asked her miserably.

"You did look a bit weird . . . and Zara was there. She's probably telling everyone you've been carted off and locked up in an attic somewhere." Ruby sighed, and then gave Lottie a hug. "I'm really, really glad you're OK. Please don't do that again for a while, all right?"

"I'll try," Lottie promised. "But I didn't do it, Ruby. It just happened." She was silent for a second. "I was scared too."

Ruby wriggled an arm round her shoulders. "So it was a new thing?" she asked, sounding curious and a little puzzled. "Why did it happen? Do you know?"

Lottie shook her head and a little shiver ran through her, making Ruby hug her tighter. "I don't know what's going on. Sofie and I went there in a dream – we even saw the same unicorn, but he galloped away when he saw us. We scared him, I think. But it was different this time. I'm sure he was running to me, as though he wanted me to help. And I did try, but then I woke up, and I don't know what's going on." She gulped. "I'm scared to go back."

Uncle Jack arrived to pick Lottie up in his van, and Lottie walked wearily out of school with him, waving to Ruby, who was making *call me* signs behind Mrs Taylor.

"I didn't think she was going to let you go," Uncle Jack muttered. "How many forms do I have to sign to take my own niece home?" They were out of the school gates now and he looked down at her worriedly. "Lottie, what happened? Sofie and your dad practically had kittens. Oh, yes, sorry, bad joke," he muttered, when Lottie sniggered. "You can't be that ill then. What's going on? Your teacher sounded pretty worried about you. I had to promise to take you to the doctor."

"I got run over by a unicorn and everyone thinks I'm going crazy," Lottie complained, trying to cheer Uncle Jack up a bit, but it only made him scowl at her anxiously. When they got to the van Sofie flung herself out of the open window into Lottie's arms.

"Lottie! Bad girl, what have you been doing without me?" she demanded, wriggling furiously in Lottie's arms as she tried to sniff and lick her all over. "Are you all right? What did that great black monster do to you? And why did you not take *me*?" She nipped one of Lottie's fingers with her sharp little white teeth as she said this, and Lottie winced.

"I didn't do anything!" she protested. "It just happened. I think he called me," she added slowly. The idea had been growing ever since she'd woken up, and she was almost sure it was right. "Like Dad said my magic called him home. That black unicorn is linked to Dad, isn't he? Because he was caught in Pandora's spell too."

Lottie realized that Uncle Jack and Sofie were both staring at her sceptically. "Well, I don't know! I'm just the one who fainted in the middle of assembly so my whole school thinks I'm totally weird; you could be a bit nicer!"

Uncle Jack leaned over her to put her seatbelt on for her, as if she were an invalid, and Sofie snuggled on to her lap as they drove away, but there was a worried silence in the van.

Lottie's dad was waiting impatiently outside the shop when they got home, so Uncle Jack dropped Lottie and Sofie off before he drove round to the yard at the back of the shop. Lottie's dad grabbed her and hugged her tight enough to hurt.

"What happened?" He held her away from him, scanning her face as though he wanted to see that she wasn't marked. "Lottie, I wanted to come, but Jack said the school wouldn't let me take you; they don't know about me. Which is stupid, as I'm your father, but probably true. I hate this!" he added angrily. "What happened?"

He half-carried Lottie inside and sat her on the counter, like she was almost sure she remembered him doing when she was little. It was odd how that now his memories had returned, her own buried memories of her childhood here were coming back too.

"I went back to the rainforest, like Sofie and I did on Saturday night," Lottie explained, rather wearily, feeling grateful that Sofie was nestling closely on her lap. "But it felt like I was pulled there. I wasn't exploring like before; I had to go somewhere." She sighed.

Sofie was standing on Lottie's legs now, her front paws reaching for Lottie's shoulders as she searched her mind. "She is too tired for this," she told Lottie's father protectively. "*I* will tell. That black unicorn, it was him who called her," Sofie muttered. "He is being chased by something, something very bad. He needs help, he calls Lottie. But he is a stupid horse, and he frightens her. You thought *he* was chasing *you*, *ma pauvre*." She nuzzled Lottie's cheek with her own whiskery one. Then she lost her affectionate side with one of her lightning changes of mood and butted Lottie's shoulder hard. "This is why you should not go anywhere on your own! I have told you and told you!"

"Why you, Lottie?" her father murmured, frowning. "I could understand if he called me. Though frankly I'm amazed he tried summoning any of us, he's been an exile for so long."

"She is a very powerful witch," Sofie snapped at him. "We are. It is no wonder he asked her to help."

"If my magic called you back from the unicorns' forest, Dad, do you think there might be traces of it still around?" Lottie asked doubtfully. "Could that be why?"

"That sounds risky," Uncle Jack put in. He was leaning on the other side of the counter, frowning at Lottie.

Lottie nodded. She felt like curling up and hiding under her duvet. She hadn't meant any of this to happen! She hadn't known she was leaving traces of her magic all over rainforests for enormous unicorns to call on.

"It's the only answer I can think of," her dad said doubtfully.

Horace had been half asleep on his perch, but now he opened his round yellow eyes very wide, and leaned down to stare off-puttingly at Lottie.

"No one has asked the most important question of all, Lottie dear." He blinked twice and then added in a low, hooting voice, "Who – or what – was that unicorn so afraid of?"

Chapter 3

Uncle Jack insisted on Lottie going to bed, at least for a bit. Although he knew she hadn't fainted from stage fright combined with lack of breakfast, Mrs Taylor had been quite convinced that was what had happened. She had told Uncle Jack that Lottie needed to rest and he seemed quite determined that she had to, even when Lottie protested that she felt fine.

Unfortunately, she had been lying on, if not actually in, her bed for all of twenty minutes when Uncle Jack opened her door very quietly and peered round it.

Lottie closed her eyes and tried to look as though she was resting. Holding a magazine didn't make her look as though she were asleep, though.

Uncle Jack didn't seem to notice. "Lottie, I'm so sorry, I know I told you to go to sleep, but your mother just phoned."

Lottie bounced upright and Sofie stopped pretending to be asleep. "Does she want to talk to me?" Lottie asked, looking for the phone, but Uncle Jack hadn't brought it upstairs.

He shook his head. "No. It was a quick call. Lottie, she was at the airport."

Lottie stared at him. "You mean . . . she's coming home now?"

"Apparently your last phone call worried her, and she decided she had better come as soon as possible. She rang to apologize; apparently they found a tenant for her flat very quickly and she had to leave today. She'll be here this afternoon."

"What are we going to do about Dad?" Lottie yelped, and Uncle Jack nodded frantically. "Exactly. Can you come downstairs? We need to work something out."

Lottie's dad was sitting at the counter arguing with Horace. "I am not running away!" he protested. But he was packing books into a small rucksack as he said it and he looked embarrassed.

"You're scared of her." The little owl snickered.

"I don't *know* her," Lottie's father muttered sadly. "Of course I'm scared."

Lottie hugged him. "It'll be all right," she promised. But she wondered if she ought to cross her fingers as she said it. She really had no idea how her mother was going to react to finding her husband alive after all these years.

"Lottie, do you want me to stay? I don't know what to do. . ." Her father ran his fingers through his thick black hair, so that the curls stood up on end. He looked like a startled bear and Lottie had to smile.

"I think she has to know about the magic before she finds out you've come back." Lottie leaned her elbows on the counter thoughtfully. "You can't explain where you've been for eight years if you can't say anything about unicorns or spells. It would just be *I forgot* . . . I don't think she'd take that very well. And she isn't going to listen to me explaining if you're there. So you have to go. Sorry, Dad. Um, *where* are you going to go?" Lottie frowned worriedly.

"Jack spoke to Ariadne. She says I can sleep on her sofa. I think she's quite glad actually; Shadow is, um. . ." Lottie's dad paused, eyeing her, not sure how much she knew. Ariadne was Uncle Jack's girlfriend and she was teaching Lottie magic, but Lottie had hardly had any lessons over the last few weeks, as Ariadne's first familiar, her cat Shadow, was dying. Shadow and Ariadne were incredibly close and she was devastated about losing him.

"I know he's going. . ." Lottie murmured.

"Mmm. I think she needs someone else there – she's hardly been sleeping, she's so worried he might need her if she lets herself leave him. And he's desperately trying to teach Tabitha everything she needs to know before he goes."

"I should have been better about visiting them," Lottie said guiltily. "I didn't want to get in the way."

"I'm sure they wouldn't think that, Lottie. Ariadne loves you and so does Shadow, though he's so proud he'd never say so. And you know Tabitha adores you." Her father grinned. "As much as any cat ever does."

Sofie snorted. "Cats are nasty and suspicious. Although Shadow is a very good familiar, for a cat," she added sadly. "Even I will miss him. Tabitha is just a silly kitten."

Lottie stroked her, smiling. Sofie had helped Lottie rescue Tabitha, even though now she liked to pretend she'd had nothing to do with it. She disliked cats on principle. When Sofie and Lottie had found Zara and her friends teasing the skinny little stray, they'd had no idea she was magical – Ariadne said possibly Tabitha hadn't known either, a bit like Lottie. Lottie had worried about bringing Tabitha back to Grace's Pet Shop because she was just an alley cat and she wouldn't fit in, but now she was Ariadne's new familiar, a silken-furred little princess.

Spoilt like a princess, Sofie added darkly, in Lottie's mind.

And you're not? Lottie grinned at her, and Sofie stuck her pointy nose in the air.

"Are you going to be all right, Lottie?" her dad asked worriedly.

Lottie shrugged, trying to look as though she wasn't worried, but she wasn't very convincing either. "If Mum actually lets me get a word in edgeways, I don't see how she can not believe me," she told him. "But that does mean she's actually got to listen to me," Lottie admitted.

"She is not able to see past her own nose, that one," Sofie added grumpily. "If you would let me bite her, Lottie, she would listen." She eyed Lottie hopefully and sighed when Lottie shook her head.

"Horace, you'll stay and help Lottie, won't you?" Lottie's father asked, getting up and swinging his pitifully small bag of belongings on to his shoulder.

The fluffy little owl eyed him irritably. "If I must."

"We'll all help Lottie!" Fred the pink mouse scampered across the counter and struck a brave and helpful pose right in front of Horace, flourishing his tail dramatically.

Horace closed his eyes slowly and hooted, "Take it away!" His claws were twitching. He found his owl instincts very hard to resist, even though he was only owl-shaped and not a real one.

Lottie scooped Fred up in her hands and cuddled him protectively. She loved Horace, but being an owl in a shop full of mice wasn't enormously helpful. No one knew how long it

54

would take Horace to regain his strength and be able to change again.

Fred, who was amazingly self-centred, hadn't even noticed Horace. He climbed on to Lottie's shoulder and stood there proudly. "I am very good at explaining to people about magic," he pointed out. "I helped you tell Ruby, didn't I, Lottie?"

Lottie smiled. He had, but only by walking in at precisely the wrong moment and then talking to Ruby about the colour of his fur.

"Mum's going to be harder to convince than Ruby," she explained, stroking the top of his head. His fur was so silky. "She's really not into magic or anything like that. She's super-sensible."

"But I'm pink!" Fred protested. "She can't just not see me."

"Oh, I bet she can," Lottie muttered. "She never noticed you before, and you and Peach and the others weren't really all that good at staying out of the way, were you?"

Fred stared at her, his dark brown eyes liquid, and his whiskers trembling with indignation. "I am a master of disguise," he told Lottie crossly. "I can't help it if the others let me down."

There was a chorus of agitated chittering from the pink mice's cage, and Fred's friend Peach leaned down from their shelf. "Button it, Fred!" he snapped. "I had to stuff your own tail in your mouth last time Lottie's mother came, and don't pretend you don't remember."

Fred bounded off Lottie's shoulder and back up to the cage to have it out with the rest of them. Lottie shared a rueful smile with her dad as the cage suddenly filled with flying mouse bedding.

"I don't suppose I can come with you?"

Lottie's mother arrived in a taxi late that afternoon. She seemed happy to be back, but there was an uncomfortable feeling between them – the last time they'd spoken, Lottie had tried to explain to her mum that she wanted to stay at the shop, rather than going back to their old home. Her mum hadn't taken it well. Lottie knew she had to explain her reasons properly this time.

She had to tell her own mother that she was a witch.

Uncle Jack had made a huge effort with dinner and Lottie had managed to stop him adding to the recipe. He was a very good cook, but he tended to find things at the back of cupboards and throw them in for extra flavour, and in this house that could be rather dangerous.

Lottie nibbled her way through chicken pie and apple crumble, trying to eat and chat and be natural. It was tricky, though. She was sitting in between her mum and Sofie, and she felt like a wall holding them apart. Lottie could tell that her mother was horrified that Sofie sat up at the table and had her own plate (and she always insisted on the best china). Sofie was keeping up a running commentary in the back of Lottie's mind, complaining about Lottie's mother.

She is staring again! So rude! No manners! I am eating most delicately, and she will not stop sighing at me. And she is feeding her carrots to that imbecile of a rabbit.

I know. But come on, Sofie, Barney's our secret weapon. We need him to help convince her.

Lottie's mum was not really keen on pets. Rabbits were the only animals she liked – she had had a rabbit of her own a bit like Barney when she was little, so she adored him. Lottie was really hoping that he would make her mother believe. The only problem was that although Barney was a sweetheart, he was not bright. He was probably the stupidest secret weapon ever.

"Danny and I'll do the washing up," Uncle Jack said, ignoring Lottie's pleading glance and Danny's look of outrage. "You two go and catch up."

There wasn't a living room at the shop — mostly they sat in the kitchen, or in the shop itself at the big counter — so Lottie took her mum upstairs to her room. She perched on the window sill with Sofie and let her mum sit on the bed — she didn't think she could have this sort of conversation sitting next to her — not yet, anyway.

"I've been thinking about what you said on the phone," her mother began, and Lottie dug her nails into her palms. She loved her mum so much and she could see how hard it was for her to talk about all this; her mum's shoulders were drooping and she looked so tired suddenly. She was obviously psyching herself up for an argument over where Lottie lived from now on. Lottie wished she could just tell her that it didn't matter anyway — she was a witch and her dad had come back to them after all. Moving back home wasn't really the issue. But she had to let her mother talk — Mum wasn't going to listen to what Lottie had to tell her about magic until she'd said what she was determined to say.

"Lottie, I really do understand how you feel. . ."

She does not! Sofie snapped.

Sofie, shut up! If I jump down her throat now, she'll never listen to me. Lottie smiled tightly and nodded.

"Lottie, it's like I said – it isn't certain, but I'm hoping I can get my old job back. You see I can't just give that up, don't you?"

Lottie put her hand on Sofie's back, partly for comfort and partly to stop Sofie breaking into a volley of angry barks.

"I know, Mum. But can't we work something out? I talked to Uncle Jack and he said maybe you could commute – not every day, I don't mean that, but come back here for the weekends?" It felt a bit pointless, saying all this, but even though she was about to change everything, she still wanted her mum to understand how she felt.

Her mother was shaking her head already and Lottie tried not to snap at her.

"Lottie, I missed you terribly when I was away! I want you with me; I can't be your mother when I'm at the other side of the country!"

Selfish! Sofie hissed and Lottie half-agreed. But she was sure her mum really did think she was doing what was best. It was just that she was wrong.

"I know, Mum, but I love having more family! I love being here with Uncle Jack and Danny and Sofie, and you've met Ruby, you know she's my best friend." It was true – Sofie was more than a friend, after all. But Lottie knew her mum would understand missing Ruby better.

"Ruby can come and visit." Lottie's mum got up and walked over to her, crouching in front of her and Sofie, knitted together on the window sill. "Lottie, I know it's going to be hard for you and I'm so sorry I had to put you through all this. But we'll get back to normal

61

so quickly, I promise you we will."

Normal, Lottie thought sadly. *It would be like cutting my hand off. My magic would just wither away. I'd probably forget all about it and be how Dad was, all lost and miserable.*

Tell her! Sofie scratched at Lottie's leg. *This is all pointless. I told you that you would not win her over like this. Just tell her. We are wasting time.*

Lottie put her hand out and held her mum's arm. "Mum, you don't understand. There's something I have to explain. . ." Holding her, Lottie tried to feel her mother's thoughts, hoping that she could gently show her the magic, rather than having to explain with words. But it was like fighting through a fog. Her mum's mind made her feel dizzy and almost faint. Lottie leaned against her mum, breathing quickly, and tried again. But then her mum gasped and struggled away, looking at Lottie in horror.

What did we do? Sofie asked, her muzzle wrinkling in confusion.

I don't know! Lottie watched as her mum stood up and backed away from her. "Mum, what's the matter? What is it?"

But her mother was reaching for the door handle. Reaching behind her, as though she didn't dare turn her back on Lottie.

Chapter 4

Lottie's mum had said she was tired from the journey and gone to bed early. She didn't give Lottie and Sofie a chance to talk to her at all.

"Didn't go well, huh?" Danny asked Lottie, his eyebrows raised, as she stared at the doorway her mother had just disappeared through.

Lottie shook her head.

"It did not go at all," Sofie put in. "Lottie's *maman*, she did not even let us begin."

Danny raised his eyebrows. "What, she wouldn't even let you explain? I didn't think she was like that, somehow. I mean, I guess she's probably as stubborn as you, Lottie, but – hey!"

The orange Lottie had thrown at him bounced to the floor, and Danny kicked it back up into his hand. His pet rat, Septimus, appeared from the pocket of his hoodie, looking indignant.

"Don't throw things at me when I'm sleeping, Lottie Grace, or if you must, peanut brittle, please. I don't like oranges." He crawled sluggishly up Danny's arm to snooze on his shoulder.

Danny threw the orange in the air and caught it. "Thanks, Lottie. Yum."

"Was that thing with your foot magic, or can you do that anyway?" Lottie asked. She was quite glad to be distracted.

"Bit of both," Danny admitted. "I'm trying to do it without the magic, but I keep squishing the oranges. So, why wouldn't she listen?"

Lottie frowned. "I couldn't work out how to explain, so I thought I'd try and show her. But as soon as I touched her mind she went really strange and she wouldn't even let me talk to her." Lottie looked up at Danny miserably. "She ran away from me, Danny. She was scared of me."

"Oh." Danny stopped passing the orange between his hands and sat down at the table opposite her. "Um. Did you do it wrong somehow?"

Lottie shrugged, and stared at him. "How do I know? What's the right way to tell your mum you're a witch anyway? All I did was try and just touch her thoughts, so I could gently slip magic in. . ."

"Hmf. We need to hit her over the head with it, Lottie," Sofie snapped. "We slip it in, she will not believe us. She is the most everyday person I have ever met."

"Lottie, is your mum all right?" Uncle Jack came in looking worried. "I met her on the stairs and she was shivering. I hope she hasn't caught something on the plane."

"Lottie's turned her mind to jelly," Danny told him, straight-faced.

"Danny! It's not funny," Lottie wailed. "Maybe I did hurt her. What am I going to do now?"

"Back to Plan A," Danny told her. "Use words."

"Lottie, what's going on?" Uncle Jack sat down, looking confused.

"Mum went really weird when I tried to slip into her thoughts," Lottie admitted. She was a bit worried Uncle Jack might be angry. Ariadne had told her that breaking into people's minds was – well, somewhere between rude, dangerous and evil. "I thought it might be the easiest way to tell her. . ."

Uncle Jack nodded thoughtfully. "She seemed frightened of me too, just now." He stared into the middle distance, a dreadful bleak look in his eyes.

Lottie's voice felt strangled and she fought to get the words out. "I didn't mean to – oh, Uncle Jack, what have I done to her?"

"It wasn't you, Lottie," he told her sadly. "At least, I'm only guessing. But it makes sense."

"What?" Sofie demanded, her whiskers trembling with curiosity.

"Hush!" Horace snapped at her from his perch, staring anxiously at Uncle Jack.

Uncle Jack looked back to Lottie and sighed. "Pandora. Don't you think? All that time she spent trying to attack your mother's mind. Isobel must have built herself some kind of defence. I don't know why Tom and I didn't think of it before."

"But how could she? She doesn't have magic! It's like Sofie just said, she's about as far away from magic as you can get. I'm not being mean, Uncle Jack, she's just really, really . . . sensible."

Uncle Jack smiled, but it was only half a smile. "Maybe she's more magical than you think. Or maybe she's just strong, Lottie. She's had to cope on her own for a long time, and before that she had to protect herself somehow. Even though your dad tried to keep Pandora away from her, he couldn't always be there. I suppose we should have realized before that Pandora trying to break into your mum's thoughts might have changed her. But then, we hardly saw you and your mum once you moved away from Netherbridge. . ."

Lottie was staring at him now, her lips half-moving as she tried to work all this out. "Uncle Jack, when I first found out that Pandora had been Dad's girlfriend, and all that other stuff about her trying to get revenge, Ariadne did say that she thought Pandora had done something to my mum. She'd done something to her mind. Do you think it was the other way round? Pandora was trying and my mum fought her off so hard that now she can't bear magic at all?" Lottie brushed at something on her cheek, and realized that she was crying.

Sofie licked the tears away lovingly. "If she has walls in her mind, Lottie, we will push them over," she promised.

"What if we can't, ever?" Lottie asked, speaking into the soft fur of Sofie's neck, as though saying it too loud might make it true.

"Lottie." Uncle Jack took her by the arms and held her tight. "Think. You were strong enough to summon your dad out of one of Pandora's spells, when you thought he was dead for a start, and he was thousands of miles away. I couldn't do that! Don't you think I tried, all those years? Do you think I just said, *Oh, Tom's gone. Funny, he's been a while.* Years, Lottie! Evening after evening, once Danny and his mum had gone to bed, I'd sit in the shop and Horace and I would try to call him back. Nothing. But you managed it. Your mum is going to be right here next to you."

Lottie nodded shakily. She so wanted to believe him. It was just that he hadn't seen the way her mum had looked at her.

"We will talk to her tomorrow after school," Sofie announced. "And I mean *we*," she added, turning round to look Lottie in the eye, her furry little face determined.

Lottie's mum still looked exhausted at breakfast the next morning. Lottie hadn't wanted to wake her, but her mum had come downstairs anyway, and now she was eating muesli very slowly. Lottie noticed that Uncle Jack kept looking at the bag of muesli rather anxiously. It had been in the back of one of the cupboards and it didn't have a label. It looked like one of those rather expensive kinds that came in a brown paper bag from a health food shop. But it was also quite possibly hamster food.

"Don't tell her," Lottie muttered in his ear, as she went to put her cereal bowl in the sink — she'd had the sugary stuff that definitely wasn't for hamsters, though she suspected Giles, the gentlemanly hamster who lived in the shop, would think it was delicious. He was fat enough already, despite his obsession with his exercise wheel.

Uncle Jack gave her a guilty little smile, and Lottie hugged her mum quickly on her way out to school. Her mum looked up at her and smiled. She looked a little dazed, but that awful frightened, suspicious look had gone. Perhaps she had forgotten what happened? Lottie hoped so.

Her mum coming back had practically put the assembly disaster out of Lottie's mind, so she was a bit surprised when Ruby looked her up and down anxiously when they met on the bridge.

"Are you all right? You aren't going to have a vision and fall in the river on the way to school, are you?"

Lottie pretended to stagger, but stopped when Ruby went white with horror. "OK, sorry. Not funny."

"I should push you in," Ruby muttered.

"What did people say after I'd gone?" Lottie asked, thinking back to what had happened the day before.

Ruby was silent for a second.

"Go on, tell me," Lottie sighed. "Let me guess. Zara said I was crazy?"

"Sort of. She couldn't make up her mind between crazy and a total liar."

"She thinks I was putting it on?" Lottie stared at Ruby in amazement.

Ruby shrugged. "You know that in her world everything is to do with her. She thinks you were trying to spoil her assembly."

"I think I feel faint," Lottie said glumly. "I might have to go home."

"Can I come?" Ruby agreed as they turned into Netherbridge Hill and saw the groups of children heading for the school. Quite a few of them turned to look at Lottie, and she could feel the whispers swirling around them, although she couldn't quite hear. It was almost worse that way.

Funnily enough, despite the whispering, everyone who came to talk to Lottie was nice.

Lily, who'd been so miserable about the dancing, actually came and hugged her.

"Are you feeling better? My sister had a panic attack in her ballet recital and she actually fell off the front of the stage. At least you didn't do that."

Lottie smiled in relief. "I can't even remember what happened," she said. Lying was easier than she'd expected it to be. "But I don't think Mrs Taylor's going to make me stand in front of the whole school again soon, and that has to be good news." Lottie was flicking her eyes around as she chatted, though, watching for Zara. She was going to turn up and be unbelievably horrible at some point – it was just a case of waiting for when, and Lottie really didn't like waiting.

It didn't happen until morning break. Zara had glared at her across the classroom every time she looked up, but they hadn't been close enough to speak without Mrs Taylor hearing. When the bell rang, Lottie took her time putting her coat on and wrapping her scarf three times around her neck. It was a gorgeous, soft purple scarf that her mum had sent her from Paris. It felt like armour, even though it did make her worry about talking to her mum that afternoon. *Why does everything have to go wrong at once?* Lottie thought wearily. It ought to work that being worried about one thing cancelled the other one out, but it didn't. She was doubly anxious instead.

Still, she wouldn't change it. It was so weird to think back to her old life. No magic. No Sofie. No *Dad*. Just her and Mum. It had been fine at the time, even though Mum was always rushing around for work, but looking back now it seemed incredibly dull.

"You are the worst liar I've met."

Lottie jumped, jolted out of her memories, and turned to face Zara. She was already trying to breathe slowly and keep calm. She didn't want to let Zara upset her. Lottie didn't want to be upset anyway, but if she lost her temper she really didn't know what she might do. It was a bit like sitting on an unexploded bomb. Lottie giggled nervously.

Zara practically had steam coming out of her ears. Her pretty pink and white face flushed scarlet and her fists were clenched. Her little gang, lined up behind her, were looking rather worried. Zara hadn't seemed to be quite so perfect recently. The school staff had stopped automatically assuming that whatever had happened, it wasn't Zara's fault, which had been the way things went ever since Reception. It was worrying, and they exchanged quick, nervous looks with each other as they watched Zara looming over Lottie.

"So you think it's funny? I thought you liked animals, Lottie Grace. You live in that stupid pet shop, after all."

Lottie blinked. What had that got to do with anything? She stared back at Zara, quietly, and Zara's friends looked even more nervous. There was something *about* Lottie. Especially when she was so quiet. And looking at Lottie and Zara now, any teacher would say that Lottie was as innocent as a lamb and Zara was bullying her.

"You ruined our assembly. It was for charity, Lottie. Mrs Taylor didn't even do the collection at the end. Everyone took their money home and the poor dogs at the shelter didn't get anything." Zara's voice dripped gooey sadness, but Lottie did feel rather guilty. She hadn't known that.

"I didn't mean to spoil it," she said uncomfortably.

"You didn't," Ruby told her. "It was loads better your way. I bet people would have paid not to see Zara dancing any more. Mrs Taylor should just have done the collection anyway, instead of letting her dance again. Anyway, you couldn't help feeling – er – faint. . ."

Zara glared at her. "She wasn't faint!" she

snapped. "You know it as well as I do, Ruby. She made the whole thing up. It was just a massive stunt to get Lottie all the attention, same as always."

"What?" Lottie murmured, staring at Zara. The Lottie that Zara was talking about didn't sound like anyone she knew. She liked staying quietly in the background. *Not* getting any attention was more what she was aiming for.

"She didn't do it on purpose," Ruby insisted. But she jabbed Lottie in the ribs with her elbow, as though to suggest that some help might be nice, rather than Lottie just standing there like a wide-eyed lemon.

"Honestly, I just felt weird," Lottie told Zara. It was true, after a fashion, which helped her to look as though she meant it.

"You're just desperate for attention," Zara told her, assuming a lofty tone of voice. She folded her arms and stared pityingly down at Lottie. "I think it's because she hasn't got a dad, and her mother went off to France and abandoned her. No one to love poor little Lottie. She has *issues*." She murmured this to Bethany, but it was obviously meant for Lottie to hear.

Usually, Lottie and Ruby would have looked at each other at this point and rolled their eyes in disgust. It would have been funny, Zara pretending to know all about it. But today it wasn't funny at all. Zara had got it all unbelievably wrong and terribly right at the same time.

Lottie's mouth moved, but she didn't say anything. She didn't even know what she wanted to say. She gulped and blinked in a desperate effort not to burst into tears.

Bite her! It was Sofie's warm, chocolate-scented presence speaking in her mind, and Lottie sniffed and smiled to herself. To Sofie.

"You know what you are?" Ruby was standing shoulder to shoulder with Lottie, scowling at Zara. "Pond slime. All of you. Especially you lot for sticking with *her*. Do you actually like being her evil little sidekicks? Or do you just not have enough brains to think for yourselves?"

"Shut up, Ruby," Bethany muttered.

"Imaginative," Ruby commented. Lottie got the feeling she was starting to enjoy herself. *Her hair gets curlier when she's angry,* she thought to herself, in a strange, dreamy way. A thudding, thundering noise was starting to echo in her blood, and the air was turning greenish and misty.

"Lottie!"

"Ugh, she's doing it again. Great. So this is what we're going to get every time anyone says something poor little Lottie doesn't like." But Zara's voice had a worried edge to it, as though she had a feeling that making someone pass out might be hard to explain.

Lottie could feel arms around her now, and someone was walking her away, pushing her to sit down.

"Lottie. Lottie! Snap out of it. Come back! You can't do this now! If you keep doing this at school they'll send you to hospital, and then they'll want to find something wrong with you, and it'll all be a disaster. Lottie, wake up!"

Lottie shook herself, brushing the strands of mist away from her mind, letting the thundering hooves die away to nothing. She couldn't help feeling that she shouldn't wake up – that something urgent was going on. That she *should* listen. But she couldn't, not right now. Ruby was right. Lottie stopped staring into nothing and looked at Ruby.

"Sorry." She rubbed her hands over her eyes hard, as though to scrub the vision away. "You're right, it wouldn't be a good idea. I didn't do it on purpose, but at least I managed to get out of it when you called me."

"Why do you think it happened again?" Ruby asked her curiously.

Lottie shrugged. "Maybe because I was trying to get away? Perhaps it was the only place I could go."

Chapter 5

Lottie's mother wasn't anywhere downstairs when Lottie got home from school. She and Sofie climbed the stairs to her room, Lottie feeling every step as though her legs had been weighted with tiredness. She pushed the door open, imagining the softness of her bed and wondering if she could get away with a little rest before she went and found her mum.

"You must not," Sofie said sternly. "If you do not do it now, you will never do it. *Rrrrr!*" The fur on the back of her neck suddenly stiffened and stood up, and Lottie looked round sharply, to see her mother sitting on the window sill gazing quietly at her.

"You made me jump," Lottie laughed nervously as she crossed the room and leaned against the window next to her mum.

Go on! Sofie snapped. *Tell her now.* Lottie's fingers tightened on her neck.

"Lottie, what's the matter?" Her mother was staring at her closely. "You look awful. So tired, and you've got great purple shadows under your eyes."

"I'm all right," Lottie muttered. "I had a bad day at school, that's all."

"What happened?" Lottie's mum wrapped her arms around her and Lottie leaned her head against her shoulder. It felt good.

"There's this horrible girl. Zara. She hates me. Ruby too."

"She's bullying you?" Lottie's mum sat up sharply and turned Lottie to face her, staring at her with worried eyes. "Has this been going on for a while? Oh, Lottie, why didn't you say?" She frowned. "This is the sort of thing I should have been here for. I should have known. I'm sorry, Lottie. I'll come up to the school tomorrow and talk to your head teacher.

Uncle Jack mentioned something today about you fainting yesterday at school. I couldn't believe it; you've never fainted. Is it all because of this girl?"

"I can deal with it myself," Lottie whispered. Her mum hugged her tighter, and Lottie could feel her mum's quick breathing on her hair. "Mum, I didn't mean to upset you yesterday. When you ran away downstairs, why was that?"

Her mum stared at the floor. "I don't know, Lottie. I was frightened of something. It was so strange; it felt as though it was something you had done, but you were nowhere near me. And how could I be frightened of you? It was like something from an awful dream, or a memory I'd shut away somewhere. It was horrible." She shivered and snuggled closer to Lottie, as though even thinking of it scared her. In that moment, Lottie loved her so much, even though it made her feel scared too. Mothers weren't supposed to be frightened of things. They were the ones who chased away the monsters under the bed.

"It was real," Sofie said darkly, and Lottie didn't realize for a second that she'd spoken aloud, until she felt the warmth of her mother's cheek lifted away from her hair. She looked up and saw her mum staring down at her and Sofie.

Lottie's mum blinked.

Sofie glared back at her. "You heard, no? It is not polite to answer?"

Lottie's mum looked at her so helplessly that Lottie laughed. She *had* heard. In that moment of closeness, when Lottie's mother wanted to protect her, and Lottie had been worrying about her too, they had broken through. They had been feeling close enough to each other that Sofie had been able to make her mother hear.

I am extremely clever, Sofie thought smugly. *But then you knew this. You should have let me organize this all along.*

"This is to do with what happened last night, isn't it?" Lottie's mother asked, her voice shaky and small. "That strange feeling. . ." She frowned. "As though something was stealing into my thoughts."

Lottie put a hand on her mother's cheek, patting it gently. "I'm sorry. I couldn't work out how to tell you and I tried to show you instead, by putting it into your mind. But you wouldn't let me."

"She talks," Lottie's mum murmured, watching Sofie in disbelief.

"*She* is the cat's pyjamas," Sofie said with her nose in the air. She sometimes came out with the strangest phrases. Lottie could tell she was enjoying the effect she was having.

"So . . . when you were trying to put thoughts into my head, Lottie . . . what exactly were you trying to tell me?" Lottie's mother dragged her eyes away from Sofie to stare at her daughter.

Lottie took a deep breath. "Well. Sofie can talk. You know that now. . . But it isn't just that.

She's magic. A magic dog."

"Deeply magic," Sofie agreed, nodding importantly. "I am very good at it." She leaned forward to address Lottie's mother, very seriously. "It is why I drink so much coffee. I need it, you see."

"Oh." Lottie's mum nodded.

"All the animals in the shop are magic, Mum," Lottie burst out. "Uncle Jack is too, and Danny, and Uncle Jack's friend Ariadne." She gulped. "And I am too. I'm a witch. Or I will be soon. Ariadne is teaching me."

"Us," Sofie pointed out.

"Us," Lottie agreed. "Sofie is my familiar."

"Not a cat?" Lottie's mum asked. Her voice sounded very thin and faint, as though she hardly believed what was going on.

"Of course not a cat!" Sofie snapped. "What would Lottie want *un chat* for when she has me? Bah!"

"Her English gets worse when she's cross," Lottie explained. "Sofie is from Paris, Mum.

She told me about it when you were there. I used to imagine you walking down the streets when she told me the names of the shops. Ariadne has cat familiars," she added. "But it just depends on the person. Danny has that black rat, Septimus, and I think Horace is Da—" Lottie gasped, and stopped.

Her mum blinked at her. "What were you going to say?" she asked slowly. "Lottie, tell me, please."

Lottie looked at her, holding her mum with her eyes. "Mum, I inherited this. Uncle Jack has it, and Danny. It came to me from Dad."

Her mother seemed hardly to be breathing. "He could do this?" she murmured. "When we lived here, the shop was like this? Magic?"

Lottie nodded. "It's what he and Uncle Jack did. Sell magical animals."

"But . . . how could I not know?" Lottie's mum was staring into space, and Lottie could tell that she was reviewing her memories, trying to find clues, search out signs. Trying to change everything – or perhaps not to.

"I – I think he would have wanted to tell you." Lottie felt her mother stare at her sharply. "Ariadne remembers him. She told me some things." Lottie was thinking quickly, trying not to let out the truth about her dad still being alive. Not yet. Not all at once. "There was – still is, actually – another witch. An enchantress called Pandora. She used to be in love with Dad, before he met you."

Her mum nodded. "I know. His old girlfriend. She was a bit odd. I met her a couple of times. She was a witch?" She laughed, but it was an odd, hard noise. "That explains quite a lot."

"She has two very skinny dogs. Ugly things. They are much too tall." Sofie sniffed.

"She was really upset when they split up. She tried to do things to you." Lottie put her hand on her mother's. "I think it was her that you remembered, trying to do things to your mind, when you felt me doing it."

"I can't believe all this," Lottie's mother murmured. "Your dad was lying to me, all that time."

"No!" Lottie shook her head fiercely. "No, I know he wanted to tell you. He wanted you to be a part of it all, but Pandora messed with your mind so much that you didn't want see what was going on."

But her mother was shaking her head, as though it hurt.

Lottie suddenly grabbed her hand again and pulled her up. "Come on. Come and see downstairs. Please. It's so wonderful, Mum, I want to show you."

Her mother smiled and nodded. It was only a small smile and she was obviously having to force herself, but she was trying. "Even though all this is completely crazy, it does feel right somehow." The smile grew a little. "I feel like this is who you're meant to be,

Lottie. I was so scared — I thought I was losing you. But it was more that you were finding yourself."

Uncle Jack was sitting at the counter, examining Fred's tail. The little pink mouse was staring over his shoulder at it anxiously.

"It's got a kink in it. I know it has! Look, it isn't right, I can tell. I think I slept on it funny. Oh, it's never going to be the same again, is it?"

Uncle Jack murmured something Lottie couldn't hear and Fred jumped away crossly. "It is not fine! It's probably broken! I need a bandage at least, and extra sunflower seeds to keep my strength up — oh!" He caught sight of Lottie's mother and clapped his paws across his mouth in horror, his eyes bulging.

Lottie's mum followed her slowly into the shop and sat down limply on one of the stools by the counter. "The mice talk too, then?" she asked Lottie, in a weak voice.

Uncle Jack unfroze and beamed at Lottie. "You told her!"

Lottie shook her head. "Sofie got sick of waiting for me to do it."

Sofie scrabbled from Lottie's arms on to the counter and sat down in the china ornament pose she used when she was particularly proud of herself. "I was right, as usual," she said complacently.

Fred tiptoed across the counter and peered up at Lottie's mum. "I don't like to criticize," he told her seriously. "But you said, *the mice talk too*, and that's quite wrong. We are absolutely the best at talking. We talk *all the time*. It isn't just that we talk *too*, not at all. You being here has been positive torture for us, it really has. I considered sewing my lips together. I'm having terrible problems with my tail and I think it could be to do with stress, from all the not talking." He peered round at it again sadly.

"H–have you tried cod liver oil?" Lottie's mother stammered. She was clearly thrown by talking to a mouse, and it seemed to be the first thing she could think of to say.

Lottie shook her head desperately while trying not to laugh, and Uncle Jack sank his head into his hands.

Fred stared up at her, enthralled. "Cod liver oil? No! What is it? Tell me all about it." He pulled up a small jar of Uncle Jack's new Classy Coat Conditioner and sat on it, arranging his tail prettily around his knees. "It sounds *fascinating.*"

There was a delicate scrabbling noise, accompanied by excited squeaks, as the rest of the pink mice hurried down from their shelf, eager to hear about this new thing.

Lottie's mum gave her a worried glance.

"They're all total hypochondriacs," Lottie whispered in her ear. "Although Fred's the worst. Sorry, Mum, but you're going to be there for hours and you'll probably end up agreeing to be their cod liver oil supplier."

Now that the rest of the animals in the shop had realized that they could talk again, the noise level went from a hushed whisper to an excited hum, and lots of creatures climbed out of their cages to come and have a proper look at Lottie's mother.

Giles the hamster stomped along his shelf and leaned down to introduce himself. "Good afternoon, ma'am. Name of Giles. How do you do?"

"How do you do?" Lottie's mother whispered back. "Er, have you lived here long?"

"No, no, a few weeks only. Delightful situation. Excellent company, good fighting. Sorry, must dash, I'm in the middle of my exercise routine, you know. Must keep on top of the old paunch; us hamsters are very prone to piling on the ounces."

Lottie's mother nodded feebly and turned back to the line of pink mice who were now standing on her hand, demanding to know exactly which bit of a cod the liver was, and indeed, what was a cod? They weren't at all sure about the idea of eating bits of

94

fish middle. Plus, was the oil very oily? Oil could be bad for the complexion, as they were sure she knew.

Lottie left her to it, and went to a small, cosy hutch that was set on a shelf across from the counter. Peering out from it anxiously with enormous, round brown eyes was Barney the rabbit.

"Hello, Barney," Lottie said gently, opening the door of the hutch. Very few of the cages in the shop were properly closed; they just looked that way to keep the non-magical customers happy. But Barney liked his closed. He was rather a nervous rabbit.

"She understands now? The nice lady?" He was watching Lottie's mother, half-hopeful, half-frightened.

Lottie nodded. "Yes, and you can talk to her now too."

"She might not like me if I talk," Barney murmured. "I'm not clever like those mice."

"She adores you," Lottie reassured him.

"And you don't have to talk to her if you don't want to. She just loves holding you and feeding you carrots."

"I like carrots," Barney agreed solemnly, and he let Lottie pick him up and carry him across the room.

Her mother looked up, smiling in sudden delight, and gently lifted the line of arguing mice off her arm. She reached out her hands to Barney almost in relief — as though here at last was something she understood.

"Oh, Lottie," she said quietly. "You knew he would persuade me. I can see now what you were fighting for all this time, wanting to stay here." She gave a deep, shaky sigh. "I don't see how I can take you away from this. It isn't just your family — it's who you are. But . . . I don't know if I can stay, Lottie. There are so many memories here, all half-buried. I've been trying to think, and you must be right that someone's been playing with my mind. I can hardly remember anything properly about our time here. Except that now I know your father was lying to me." Her voice shivered. "I can't believe it still. . . . He was so trustworthy. Even when I hated him for leaving us, I still loved him. I think. . ."

Lottie stared at her, watching her mother's eyes filling with tears. This was so unfair. She knew that her father had loved them both, but it had been hard for her to believe it too. And Lottie hadn't lived with what must now seem like a lie for years.

Sofie nudged her lightly and Lottie looked down. Sofie's eyes were glowing with excitement. *Do what you did to your father!* she told Lottie. *She will let you touch her mind now, I'm sure. Show her a memory. Prove he loved you.*

Lottie nodded, swallowing nervously. She had shared several of her father's memories of herself as a young child now, and there was one that she knew would be perfect. She put her hand lightly on her mother's as she stroked

Barney, and closed her eyes.

They were in the kitchen of the shop, sitting at the same table that was there now. Even the plants were the same, the red geraniums on the window sill. Now in November there were only a few scarlet petals clinging on, but this was a summer memory and the flowers blazed.

Lottie was sitting on one of the kitchen chairs, but her chin hardly reached up to the tabletop – she was tiny. She was laughing delightedly, watching Horace, who was perched on the teapot. He was a parrot already, and the older Lottie realized sadly that this must mean she was remembering the last few weeks that her father and mother had been together.

They had their arms around each other, smiling lovingly down at Lottie, who was feeding sunflower seeds to Horace and gigging hysterically as he spat out the shells all over the table.

"You remember all this?" Lottie's mother whispered, and Lottie nodded. It was half-true. She did feel as though she remembered it. She knew what happened next, that Horace accidentally spat a shell that hit her on the nose, and she howled, and her father scooped her up and made her laugh again by blowing raspberries on her tummy. It was her memory now.

"He loved you so much," Lottie's mother murmured, and Lottie wanted to yell, *You too!*

We should let him tell her, Sofie murmured, and Lottie stood up. Sofie leapt athletically down from the counter and together they went to the door, Lottie grabbing her coat from the hook on her way.

Lottie paused and looked back as she put her hand on the door handle. "I won't be long," she whispered as she watched her mother raising Barney to her tear-stained cheek to rub against his soft coat and saw the rabbit's blissful face. Her mother nodded, looking dazed still.

They ran to Ariadne's. Sofie, for once, didn't complain or beg to be carried. She raced through the streets, pulling Lottie on.

Lottie was all set to hammer on the door, but as they reached the street where Ariadne had her pretty flat, she saw her father walking towards her in the half-darkness, striding along, his shoulders hunched in his battered yellow mackintosh and his expression eager.

"I could feel you, Lottie," he explained, hugging her tightly. "Did you try to call me?"

Lottie shook her head. "No. Well, I didn't mean to anyway. But I was coming to find you, so maybe you felt that. Dad, she's at the shop. . ." Lottie looked up at him anxiously. "I think you should come back. I told her about me." She laughed, with half a sob buried in the sound. "Just before I left she was talking about alternative remedies to

Fred. She doesn't even believe in all that stuff, only multivitamins. . . Dad, you have to talk to her. She doesn't know what to think, she feels like you lied to her all that time. I can't tell her that you're still alive. You need to come now!"

Her father held her tighter and said nothing. Lottie could almost feel the thoughts and hopes and fears flying through his mind. Then he stood up straighter, keeping one arm around her shoulders, and stepped forward, a huge stride, as though he was setting out on another journey.

Chapter 6

Lottie and Sofie walked as far as the shop with Lottie's dad, but then Lottie drew back at the door.

"What is it?" her dad asked. He had his hand on the door handle and there was an expression on his face that Lottie had never seen, one of almost painful eagerness. He was holding himself back to talk to her.

"I think you ought to go in without me," Lottie explained. She was talking to herself as much as to him. She hadn't planned this. But suddenly she felt as though her mum and dad should meet again without her there.

Her dad nodded slowly. "Yes . . . maybe you're right. Wish me luck, Lottie," he muttered in her ear as he quickly kissed her cheek. Then he pushed the door open sharply, before he could change his mind.

The bell jangled and then the door shut behind him, and Lottie stood on the step outside, trying not to peer through the window. It was so hard to resist. She caught a quick glimpse of her mother standing up with the most amazing expression of joy and hope and sheer terror all mixed together, and then Lottie dashed away, Sofie galloping after her.

It was cold and really dark now, and Lottie stopped at the end of the street, wondering where to go. She couldn't just turn up at Ruby's – Ruby wouldn't mind, but her mum might. She decided to go and see Ariadne, half-running through the streets and wishing she'd thought to bring her scarf and hat instead of just throwing a coat on. It was *freezing*.

"Lottie, if you carry me, we will both be warmer," Sofie suggested plaintively, swarming round her legs, and Lottie picked her up, snuggling the dachshund into the front of her coat like a furry hot water bottle.

Ariadne took a while to answer the door and Lottie had started to worry that she was out. She turned away, wondering if it would be all right to go home if she walked slowly. But then she heard the lock click and Ariadne was standing there, her pale face whiter than Lottie had ever seen it.

"Oh no. . ." Lottie murmured, and Sofie whined in sympathy. "Has Shadow. . .?"

Ariadne nodded, stiffly, as if she felt she might overflow if she moved too fast. Then she stood back to let Lottie in.

Lottie crept over the threshold. Apart from having a father who had died, and then finding out that he hadn't at all, she didn't have much experience with death. She couldn't help glancing around the room, wondering where he – it – was. He wasn't really Shadow any more.

"He's lying on my bed, Lottie," Ariadne said wearily, and Tabitha, who was coiled in her arms, moaned very slightly. She looked as worn as her mistress, all huge green eyes in a thin little striped face.

"You can go and see him, if you like."

Lottie hesitated. She didn't want to. But she could feel that Sofie did.

"Yes." Sofie was silent a moment. "We were − not enemies, but not friends either. But we had known each other a long time. I would like to say *adieu*."

Shadow looked strangely small, lying on a velvet scarf of Ariadne's. His eyes were sunken under their lids and his glossy black fur had a dusty tinge. Lottie had never known him when he was young, but she had seen her father's memories of the athletic jet-black cat who loved to climb trees. She blinked back tears.

Sofie put her paws on the edge of the bed and rested her muzzle on the bedcover, staring at Shadow with fiercely glinting eyes. *Goodbye*, she whispered to him silently and then she jumped down, butting her smooth head into Lottie's hand.

Come on, Lottie. He does not need us, but Ariadne and that silly girl-cat do.

Ariadne and Tabitha were curled on the smart purple sofa in the living room of the flat and Ariadne was gazing at the strange, silver-framed mirror opposite them. But she wasn't seeing it. Lottie thought she was probably seeing Shadow, Shadow alive and young and happy.

Tabitha looked scared. She had always been thin, but today her thinness made her seem frail and frightened, rather than wiry.

She has no Shadow to tell her what it is she must do, now, Sofie pointed out to Lottie. *She is the responsible one. And she has to break Ariadne out of this – this black fog she is in.* She jumped out of Lottie's arms on to the sofa and delicately touched noses with Tabitha.

Lottie blinked. This was most unlike Sofie, who normally whiled away their time in Ariadne's flat with unsubtle comments about how unfortunate the cats made it smell.

Tabitha stared back at her miserably and Sofie settled down next to the little cat, their sides touching.

Lottie, sit with us! she commanded crossly. *I am not big enough to hold Ariadne too. Hold her hand. Or pat her. Something.*

Lottie sat down obediently, glad that Sofie was taking charge. She wasn't sure she knew what to say. She leaned against Ariadne's shoulder and the witch smiled down at her gratefully.

"I'd had him so long," she said quietly, and Lottie nodded. "If I lost Sofie. . ." she whispered, shivering. "And I've only known her for four months."

They sat silently, all thinking about Shadow. Ariadne was sharing her thoughts with Lottie and Sofie as well as Tabitha, remembering being about Lottie's age, and being given the most wonderful present. The mirror in front of them misted over and then cleared, showing a red-haired girl, and in her arms a tiny black kitten. Lottie had never seen anyone looking so happy.

"What if you hadn't liked him?" Lottie whispered. "I mean, if he wasn't the right familiar for you? Who gave him to you?"

"My mother. My aunt was a witch too, and her cat had kittens. Shadow was one of them. My mother chose him for me – I suppose she knew me well enough to choose." Ariadne held Lottie closer for a minute, feeling her sigh. "I'm sorry. That was a thoughtless thing to say."

"I've told my mum now." Lottie smiled. "I can't imagine having a witch for a mum. Did you learn magic when you were tiny? Did you just always know it?"

"Some of it, I suppose. It was part of my life. But Lottie, this is amazing. You told her? She understands?"

Sofie sniffed. "She is not an understanding person. I told her, *en effet*. Lottie was too nervous. But I do not think she really knows yet what it all means. Perhaps she never will."

Lottie sighed again, even more heavily this time. "I don't know. It's a start that she can hear everyone at the shop. I can hardly believe we managed that even. And I think – I hope – that now she understands a little, she won't try to make me leave. She just couldn't."

Ariadne nodded. "And your dad? He's gone to see her? He just threw his coat on and raced out, told me he was sorry, but he had to go, you needed him for something. I would have tried to help, but I could feel that Shadow was – was slipping away from me. . . He died a few minutes after your father left, and then I'm afraid I forgot. . ."

"Yes, he's gone to talk to her. To try and explain. You look exhausted," Lottie told her gently. "Couldn't you sleep?" She knew Ariadne had hardly dared to leave Shadow for weeks now.

Tabitha purred, a tiny little purr of encouragement, her green eyes gazing hopefully at Lottie. Clearly she was desperate for Ariadne to let herself rest.

"Mmm." Ariadne sighed, letting Tabitha knead soft paws lovingly against her shoulders and closing her eyes for a moment. "So much to do. . ." she muttered, fidgeting slightly, but Tabitha purred louder, and Ariadne's breathing slowed and settled.

The purring was hypnotic, and Lottie felt her eyes closing too. She was exhausted with the strain of the last couple of days. A soft, violet mist seemed to drift in front of her eyes, and she snuggled against the sofa cushions, with Sofie coiled blissfully into her lap and Tabitha's whiskers brushing her cheek.

Curled together, the two witches and the dog and the cat drowsed, lost in a warm, magical sleep.

A shrill scream, a horse's scream, echoed through the room, and Lottie twitched in fear. She opened her eyes slowly and found that she and Sofie were curled into a soft, mossy hollow of a fallen tree. It was evening, she thought, seeing the mists gathering between the enormous tree trunks. She could hear the river close by and a dull roar that must mean a waterfall. A tiny red frog was staring at her from between the moss stems, its round eyes looking comically surprised.

"Do not touch it," Sofie hissed. "It must be poisonous, to be that colour."

Lottie nodded, pulling back her hand, and the frog stared back innocently. Then it dived off the tree, disappearing into the growing dusk.

"We frightened it off," Lottie said sadly. She would have loved to talk to a dream-frog.

"Not us," Sofie muttered, staring away through the trees, and Lottie gasped. For a moment or two, the beauty of the forest had made her forget that eerie scream. Now she followed Sofie's pointing muzzle, feeling the ground shake with the beat of hundreds of hooves.

"Something is chasing them again," Sofie told her, her paws scratching nervously at Lottie's arm. "This is not right. They are not just running, like horses run sometimes, like I run, for the sake of the speed. This is flight. They are terrified."

"I can't even see them," Lottie whispered.

"Nor can I," Sofie agreed. "But I can feel. The whole forest is full of it. Can you not feel it, Lottie?" And she turned to look at Lottie, her huge black eyes fearful.

Lottie nodded. There was no other noise above the thud of hooves, no bird calls. Even the trees seemed frozen as the unicorns galloped on towards Lottie and Sofie.

"What are they so scared of?" Lottie whispered. "Horace asked me that, when I dreamed of the black unicorn at school. I didn't do anything about it. I just forgot. . . It seemed like a dream, but it isn't. . . I've wasted all that time."

"You were doing other things. Important things. And we are here now." Sofie rubbed her cheek quickly across Lottie's hand. "Although . . . I do not know what we are going to do."

Now at last they could see the unicorns, flowing eerily through the trees towards them. So many! Lottie thought there must be fifty at least, silver and golden and white. And last of all, towering over the others, the black unicorn, shepherding them all to safety.

At least, that was what it looked like. Lottie stood up on the tree trunk, with Sofie posed proudly in her arms. This time she didn't want to hide. She still didn't know why she was here, but it had to be for a reason.

The black unicorn put on a massive turn of speed, the rest of the herd parting as he galloped through to Lottie and Sofie.

Somehow Lottie knew what he wanted her to do, though she had never thought she would dare. As he slowed and drew towards them, she reached out and seized a handful of his dark mane. It felt warm and rough under her fingers and she gripped it tightly, wrapping it over Sofie as she scrambled on to the black unicorn's back, crouching low over his neck.

Immediately he swung away again, leading the herd through the trees to the more open ground by the river. Lottie could feel his muscles bunching and moving underneath her as he bounded forward. It was like sitting on the back of some amazingly powerful engine. They were surrounded by a galloping tide of white, silver and gold, the hooves thudding in unison. It should have been the most wonderful feeling, and in a way, it was. But flooding through the herd was an undercurrent of terror. As Sofie had said when she felt them coming, they weren't just running, they were running *away*.

Lottie curled her fingers tighter in the jet-black strands of the unicorn's mane, and risked a glance behind her. She took a deep, frightened breath and looked forward again, towards the river. "Faster," she whispered.

Dark figures were slinking after them through the trees.

The unicorns slowed slightly as they reached the bank, and the black stallion looked round at Sofie and Lottie. "Are you ready?" he asked. It was the first time they had heard his voice, deep and soft and wild. He sounded unused to talking, and Lottie remembered sadly that he had exiled himself from the herd after he had been captured in Pandora's spell. He must have returned to help them fight this new threat.

It was Pandora again. It had to be.

Lottie nodded, and the unicorns leapt into the river – not dashing through the shallows, as Lottie and Sofie had watched the black unicorn do before, but straight into the deep central channel, swimming strongly for the far bank of the river.

The water dragged at Lottie's legs and she wondered nervously if there were crocodiles here, hugging herself closer to the satin back.

"I do not like to get wet," Sofie muttered furiously, shaking her ears and burrowing herself underneath Lottie.

"Be thankful for the water," the unicorn gasped back, all his strength going on fighting the current.

Lottie looked back again. They were there now, on the bank of the river. Three dark figures whose faces she could hardly see. Some magic was hiding them from her. But there was a flash of white-blonde hair as the figure in front turned angrily away.

This time, Pandora had come herself.

Chapter 7

"Why did the water stop them?" Lottie murmured, and opened her eyes. "Oh!"

She was curled on the purple sofa, her fingers wound into a fluffy cushion cover. Sofie was sitting beside her, blinking in confusion. Ariadne and Tabitha sat watching her anxiously.

"Who were they?" Ariadne asked, standing up quickly and putting her arms round Lottie. "Are you all right? We could only see flashes of what was happening. Was that Pandora?"

Lottie nodded, sitting up and wriggling her shoulders. She ached as though she had been hunched up – crouched over the shoulders of an enormous horse.

"I think it was. I saw her hair. But I don't know who the other two were."

Ariadne shook her head. Her eyes were wide and worried. "Lottie, I don't understand. Where were you? Your father told me about the unicorns and I wanted so much to believe him – he seemed so certain. But I don't understand how you were there too."

Sofie and Lottie exchanged glances. "We don't understand it properly either," Lottie said, shrugging wearily. "It's something to do with me being linked with Dad – my magic being almost a part of his, because I inherited it from him. We spent all that time dreaming of him, when he was in the rainforest, and calling him home. Now we can go back there sometimes, even though he isn't there any more."

"But we are called back there," Sofie put in. "Lottie does not choose to go. It just happens."

"You saw the black unicorn?" Lottie asked, and Ariadne nodded eagerly.

"He was wonderful – the most beautiful creature I've ever seen." She cradled Tabitha lovingly, and Lottie knew that she was silently reassuring the little cat that she actually meant, *The most beautiful creature apart from you*. . .

Tabitha purred. "He was beautiful," she agreed, in her soft little voice. "But so sad."

Lottie blinked at her, surprised that she should have seen it so easily. "When those people Pandora sent caught my dad in that spell, they caught the black unicorn too. Dad called him Midnight. Dad was with him, you see. He lost all his memories too, and he spent years hiding away from all the others. He must be terribly sad."

"And now he has come back to fight," Sofie said grimly. "He is not going to let her destroy any of the rest of the herd the same way."

Lottie shivered. "What does she want?" she asked miserably.

Ariadne held her tighter, and Tabitha and Sofie pressed against them, sending waves of love and comfort.

Ariadne's voice was very quiet, almost a breath, as she said what no one really wanted to hear.

"Revenge, Lottie. She wants revenge. She wants to destroy everything your father loves. She knows he'll try to stop her, then she'll get another chance to fight him."

There was silence for a moment, and then Lottie jumped up. "I have to go back," she said, looking wildly around the room. "She's going to do something awful to them and they can't just keep running. It won't work for ever. She's too strong, and they were getting so tired. They're so frightened, too. I have to go back and help them."

Everyone stared at her, and then Sofie shrugged. "How?" she asked pointedly. "You do not choose to go. We do not know how you go. We need Midnight. We cannot just *go*, Lottie."

Lottie sat down on the floor. "But then what can we do?" she asked helplessly. "We can't just leave them. She'll – she'll do something awful!"

Sofie nodded. "That, I agree. But we are useless, stuck here." Her tail thumped with frustration.

Ariadne stood up. "Come on. I know it isn't the best time, when your dad's trying to talk to your mum about disappearing for eight years, but this is even more important. Maybe the two of you together can work something out, and we can't lose that chance." She swept them all towards the door, hurrying Lottie into her coat and wrapping an enormous rose-pink velvet scarf over the top.

Lottie smiled at her gratefully as they hurried out to the street. "That's one of the things that made me so sure that Pandora was wrong and you were right," she muttered awkwardly.

Ariadne looked puzzled. "What? That I like pink? You were cold when you came in, Lottie; it's only a scarf."

"Mmm. And you noticed. Pandora wouldn't have cared. She doesn't care about anyone."

Ariadne frowned as they headed out into the night, the street lamps shining on the settling frost. "I know. That has to be something we can use against her somehow, Lottie. Your love for all the animals in Jack's shop saved you before. Her lack of love must be the key."

Lottie nodded. It was almost as sad as Midnight hiding away in the darkest parts of the forest, alone and ashamed. Pandora was an exile too.

"She made herself an exile, Lottie," Sofie snapped. "Do not feel too sorry for her. Or I will bite you."

Grace's Pet Shop was brightly lit against the night sky as they hurried up the little narrow street. As soon as they saw the glowing windows, everyone walked faster, eager to be part of that welcoming light. But Lottie hesitated as they reached the door, seeing two figures outlined against the glass.

Ariadne squeezed her hand. "It will be all right, Lottie. I promise. Even if they can't be together again the way you want, we will make it work out somehow. Tabitha and Sofie and I, we're not letting you go now. And nor would Jack."

Lottie nodded, smiling at her gratefully. Sometimes it was nice to let someone comfort her, instead of trying to do everything herself. She couldn't have put it all into words. She crouched down to let Sofie snuggle into her arms, then stood up, letting Sofie's unshakeable confidence flow through her.

I love you, Lottie, Sofie reminded her fiercely. *Whatever anyone says, remember that.*

Lottie buried her nose in Sofie's sweet-smelling fur for a second, breathing in Sofie's signature chocolate and vanilla scent; then she opened the door.

Her parents were sitting on either side of the counter, deep in conversation. They looked up in surprise as the bell jangled sharply.

"Lottie!" Her mother sprang up and hugged her, so hard it almost hurt, and Sofie yapped indigantly.

"Oh, Sofie, I'm sorry." Lottie's mum held out a cautious hand in apology.

"Hmf." Sofie extended her head graciously, and allowed Lottie's mum to stroke her.

"Are you – all right?" Lottie asked hesitantly.

Her mum nodded. "I think so. To be honest, Lottie, I can't think straight, after everything that's happened today. Your dad's tried to explain it all – but there's so much. . . He was just telling me that you rescued him, Lottie. That it's all down to you that he's back." She shook her head in amazement. "Lottie, I can't believe that you can do all of this, these incredible things. I thought talking animals was wonderful enough. . ."

"It wasn't that special," Lottie objected, looking embarrassed. "I didn't know I was even doing it!"

Her mother smiled at her, but the smile had a worried edge. "It's all so dangerous, though," she murmured. "Your dad's been telling me all these amazing things, but then now I look at you, you're my same daughter, and it scares me."

Lottie glanced at Ariadne, who was hanging back, trying not to get in the way.

"Pandora," her mother went on. "I can't believe you fought her, Lottie." She looked down at her hands, her face puzzled. "I want to scratch her eyes out," she confessed, stretching out her fingers and staring at them as though they didn't belong to her.

Perhaps we should take her with us, Sofie chuckled grimly.

"We've got something to tell you," Lottie whispered, looking round at Ariadne beseechingly. How could she tell her mother that they needed to go back and fight Pandora again?

"Lottie, what is it?" Her dad stood up and came over to hold her shoulders, searching her face. It was odd. He looked worried about her now, but underneath that worry, the creases seemed to have been ironed out of his face, as though he had finally allowed himself to relax. Lottie wished she had time to enjoy the sight of her parents together, for the first time in so long. It was so unfair that she had to ruin this moment.

"Lottie, are you all right?" asked her dad, cupping one hand around her cheek anxiously. Lottie looked over his shoulder and saw her mum's face, watched the pattern of emotions flickering across it: fear for Lottie, joy at seeing Lottie and her father so close and loving, the tiniest hint of jealousy – she had been Lottie's only parent for such a long time, and now she had to share again.

Lottie nodded and caught her dad's hand,

pulling him across so she could lean against her mother too – so she could join them together. "I'm fine. I'm not hurt or anything, I promise. But I went to Ariadne's, to leave you alone, to give you a chance to talk."

Ariadne moved towards them and Lottie's dad sucked in a breath.

"You're here – then, Shadow? Has he gone? Oh, Ariadne, I'm so sorry."

Uncle Jack suddenly came barging out of the kitchen – Lottie thought he had probably been tactfully hiding out of the way too. Danny followed him, looking upset at the news.

Uncle Jack hugged Ariadne and Tabitha protectively, and Ariadne clung on to him. "Jack, listen. You have to listen to Lottie," she gasped, after a few seconds.

"What is it?" Uncle Jack and Lottie's dad spoke at the same time, and then grinned at each other. All of a sudden Lottie could see how hard it must have been for her mother, shut out of this magical closeness. She squeezed her mum's hand tightly.

"We all fell asleep; Ariadne and Tabitha were upset about Shadow and so were we, and Sofie and me were really worn out after finally telling all the secrets. We just crashed out on the sofa. And then. . . It's hard to explain, but I didn't faint at school on Monday. Mrs Taylor just thought I did." Lottie sighed. "I had a vision. I went dream-travelling – to the rainforest where Dad was. I've been before in my dreams. Me and Sofie can travel in Dad's memories somehow. But it's real. Not just memories. We're there *now*. In this time, I mean, not the past."

Lottie's mum looked at her dad anxiously, as though she needed him to interpret this, but he was staring thoughtfully at Lottie.

"And I had another vision. It happened again, just now at Ariadne's – Ariadne and Tabitha saw bits of it too. I guess it was so strong it spilled over, and out of my mind. Dad, we have to go back. Pandora's there. Actually there, this time, I mean; she hasn't just sent people. It's her and two others and they're chasing the unicorns!" Lottie gulped. "I'm not sure what they want to do . . ." she added in a whisper.

"Something *monstreux*," Sofie muttered, with a shudder that shook her whole body. "She is an evil woman. We should never have let her go, Lottie. Now we have to fight her all over again." Sofie glared at Lottie's father. "So noble," she grumbled.

Lottie's dad shrugged. "It isn't that simple, Sofie. Dogs only see things in black and white. . ."

Sofie gave a contemptuous sniff. "But still we have to start again, and she has had weeks to become strong. And now there are others with her!"

"Tom, what's going on?" Lottie's mother asked. "Lottie, you can't fight her again! It's too dangerous. Lottie, please!"

Lottie put Sofie down on the counter and

put a hand on either side of her mother's face. She closed her eyes and pushed gently at the tight bindings round her mother's mind. Reluctantly at first, her mum gave in, letting Lottie share the vision of the terrified unicorns galloping headlong through the forest.

When Lottie let go, her mum swayed, her eyes wide and horrified. Lottie's dad grabbed her and held her, and Lottie's heart thumped with sudden delight. They seemed so perfect together. Maybe it would be all right.

"You can't leave them . . . I see that now. You won't, Lottie, will you, whatever I say." Lottie's mother sighed and sank back on to her stool. "You have to go back. . ."

"But I don't know how to. That's the problem!" Lottie exclaimed. "Dad, can you tell me how to make myself go there?"

"No!" her father said, so sharply that everyone jumped. "At least, not on your own, Lottie," he added more gently.

Lottie's mum looked at him, half-hopeful,

half–frightened, and he smiled at her lovingly. "You didn't think I was going to send her back there without me, did you, Isobel?" he asked.

"You've only just managed to get away," Lottie's mother murmured. "What if she traps you there again?"

"We will not let her," Sofie pointed out stoutly. "The three of us will go." Then she put her head on one side thoughtfully. "And what are we going to do when we get there?" she enquired.

Lottie opened her mouth and then shut it again, rather foolishly. "I don't know," she admitted. "We can't have a plan yet; we don't know what's happening."

"Take us with you!" Fred suggested, jumping down from his shelf in a series of dangerous leaps. "We're ever so good at improvising, us mice!" But Lottie noticed that the rest of the pink mice were gathered along the front of their cage, looking decidedly less keen. She tickled Fred's whiskers. "I would if I could, but I don't even know how to get myself there."

Her dad was frowning blackly. "There must be a way," he muttered. "Jack? Ariadne? What can we do? Lottie gets there through some link in my magic, my memories. . . . But my memories of the rainforest are so clouded."

"It can't be only your memories, now," Uncle Jack said thoughtfully. "It's like Lottie said, it's real. Your memory is only the door she's travelling through."

"Perhaps if we sent you to sleep?" Ariadne muttered, pacing up and down the shop. "If you could dream. . . No, that wouldn't work. . . ."

"The door!"

Lottie and Sofie yelled it at the same time, and everyone else jumped. Fred collapsed dramatically on Lottie's shoulder.

But then Tabitha gave a little hiss of delight. "Yesss! The door at the top of the house!"

Lottie's father's mouth dropped open. "You found that?"

Uncle Jack was frowning. "And you made

it open?"

Lottie smiled. "We went to Paris. We came to see you," she told her mum, nudging her arm gently. "It's a strange little door, and it opens – well, where you need it to, I suppose. You didn't know we were there, but you talked about me. It was when I was upset that you'd left me behind. It was so good to see you."

"You never told me!" Danny said disgustedly. "Forget school, I could have gone snowboarding!"

"That is why it would not open for you, *imbécile*," Sofie said witheringly. "It is for times of great need only. Lottie, let us go upstairs."

"Wait!" Lottie's mother gasped. "Wait, Lottie. Don't you need to pack? Or – or take anything? Please don't just go!"

Lottie hugged her. "Mum, if I don't go now and I stay here and think about it, I don't think I'll ever go," she mumbled in her mother's ear.

Lottie's father gently scooped Sofie up. "I'm coming with you. This is all my fault; I'm not letting you do this without me." He smiled at Horace. "You said I'd go back. You were right."

Horace nodded, his owl eyes huge and solemn in his fluffy little face. Then he launched himself from the counter and swooped towards the staircase. Everyone else followed him, clattering up the wooden stairs.

Sofie somehow got there first and stood staring back at everyone, her tail thumping the floorboards eagerly. In front of her was a tiny brown door, which looked perfectly innocent – except that it wasn't usually there. It only came when it was needed.

"Is that a door?" Lottie's mother asked, blinking and looking rather confused.

Lottie beamed at her. "Yes – you can see it then?"

"I think so. It's not usually there, is it? I'm not sure it's there now. . ." She reached out, brushing with her fingertips, and suddenly there was only empty air. That strange, stretched bit of wall with the unexciting little brown door had gone again.

"Oh!" Lottie's mum looked at her fingers in disappointment.

"It will come back," Sofie told her, nosing her ankle encouragingly. "See!" And she jumped up, scrabbling her little ginger paws into the air, and sure enough, the door was back again. "Come on, Lottie!"

Lottie's father grabbed her hand tightly and Lottie looked up at him. "We need to pay the door to open, do you remember? I don't know what to use. It feels like it might need more than last time. Then it was only a hair, but this time it seems so much more – risky, I suppose."

Her father smiled. "I know what to use. I found this in my coat pocket. It must have been there all along, but I only found it this morning. It can't be a coincidence. Someone knew I'd have to go back." He held out his hand, and lying in his palm was a long, black hair. Strong and thick, and shining with a mysterious gleam, Lottie knew at once what it was.

Whose it was.

"Midnight's hair!" She took it from her father's hand and touched it against the door.

There was a strange little sigh, and Lottie wasn't sure whether it was her, or Sofie, or her father, or the door opening.

Sofie raced through into the dappled shade of the forest and Lottie and her father followed, feeling the door swing shut behind them.

Chapter 8

It was odd to walk through the forest with someone else. Lottie was used to being there on her own, or with Sofie, who felt like a part of her anyway. Now she could hear her father's footsteps in the rustling earth as well as her own.

They were close to the river, just downstream from the waterfall that Lottie had heard last time. Out of the shadow of the huge trees, there were occasional bursts of sunlight, breaking through the clouds of mist flung up by the waterfall. It was huge, cascading down a dark rock face in a shower of glittering spray. Tiny jewelled birds flitted in amongst the droplets and the sun struck little rainbows where the water bounced off the rocks.

But there was no time to admire it, much as they wanted to.

Lottie turned a worried face to her dad. "How do we find them? I didn't think of that! In the dreams I've just gone to the right place."

Her father was frowning thoughtfully. "These clearings by the waterfall were one of their favourite grazing places. And there are a few other spots I think I could take us to. I remember it so much better now I'm here again!" He looked around, smiling a little, closing his eyes and feeling the sunlight on his face. Then he shook himself. "I'm sorry, Lottie. It's just that I thought I'd never come here again, and even with what happened, it's still the most magical place I've ever been to." He turned himself away from the waterfall firmly. "It would be better if we didn't have to search. Quicker. . ."

"Why can we not call *them*?" Sofie demanded. "If they can do it to us? Hmm?"

Lottie and her father exchanged thoughtful glances, and Lottie nodded. "There must be a way," she murmured, staring vaguely into the wisps of mist thrown up by the waterfall. The rare sunlight had disappeared again and the waterfall looked grander and greyer than before, shrouded in mist.

The unicorns had been like mist too, she remembered, threading through the trees, so delicate and beautiful. Lottie reached out a hand, stretching her fingers, pulling a strand of mist towards her. She twisted it into a horse shape and sent it galloping, and another, and another.

Her father smiled and did the same, and Sofie snapped at the mist unicorns, sending them on their way.

Last of all, Lottie pulled a dark thread from the hem of her school skirt and wound it around the neck of her last and largest unicorn, stroking her fingers across the thread and into the mist trails along his back so that he became a midnight unicorn, and he galloped after the others, his mist-mane streaming as he floated away.

"What if Pandora sees them?" Lottie asked her dad.

Her father sighed. "If she does, she does. To be honest, Lottie, I wouldn't be surprised if she knew we were here already. We can't do this secretly. We've come to fight." He shivered as he said it, and Lottie knew he was worried about her being there.

She nodded. She knew what he really meant – they were here not only to fight, but to win. They had to win, or she couldn't imagine what would happen. Not just to the unicorns, but to her, and Sofie, and her father. After the last fight, she didn't think Pandora would let them go if they lost.

They had taken pity on her last time. Sadly, that would probably make things worse. Lottie thought Pandora might hate losing most of all. Lottie and her father had not only defeated her, they had pitied her and *let her go*. She would not want them to survive and go telling the tale. As they walked further into the forest, Lottie realized, with a cold, sick feeling, that Pandora didn't just want to hurt the unicorns. She wanted one last chance to fight Lottie and her father. It *was* a trap; Ariadne had been right. But that didn't mean they could go home and leave the unicorns to fight the enchantress alone.

"Look!" Sofie was leaning forward, reaching out of Lottie's arms.

Quickly, Lottie turned to scan the trees, and gasped. Without them noticing, the unicorn herd had appeared at the edge of the forest, spread out in a line scattered through the trees, watching Lottie and her father cautiously.

They lit up the shadows in their white and gold, but in the centre of the line, Midnight seemed to draw the shadows closer, as if his night-dark coat was made of shadow.

He paced towards them, and Lottie shivered as she saw the shadows trail around him as he walked. The years of loneliness had not left him.

"You called us. You came back," he said to Lottie, lowering his head in front of her as though he were bowing. He still spoke slowly, as though he wasn't used to it, but this time, his voice ached with gratitude. "We didn't know if you would. We didn't dare to hope. Can you help us?"

Lottie nodded. "We want to," she told him eagerly, holding out a hand, but not sure if it was all right to touch him. He seemed so wild somehow, too special to stroke.

"He is only a fancy horse," Sofie muttered resentfully, and Midnight rolled one eye round at her in a glance of amusement.

"I like to be stroked, Lottie. Even unicorns like their noses rubbed."

Lottie petted his soft, whiskery nose and sighed. "We want to help so much, but we don't know how to. I brought my dad too. Do you remember him?"

Midnight nodded, but his ears had laid back against his skull, as though the memories Lottie's father brought were bad ones.

"I'm sorry, Midnight," Lottie's dad said quietly. "I brought this on all of you. It's only right I should be here to sort it out."

Midnight closed his eyes for a fraction of a second, then took a step towards Lottie's father and touched him with his nose. He shivered. "It wasn't you. Never blame yourself. It was her. And now she has come back."

Lottie's father didn't say anything. Instead he stroked one hand all the way down Midnight's face, from ears to nose, leaving behind a trail of glittery golden sparks. "But I am sorry, so sorry it happened that way. I'll do anything to make it up to you."

Midnight's ears trembled and pricked upright as the magic sank in. His eyes seemed brighter, and his voice held the faintest tinge of excitement. "This time, we will be ready."

"But we aren't!" Lottie protested. She flushed pink when they all turned to look at her. "At least, I'm not. . ."

Sofie licked her cheek. "You are. I am, and you are too. You'll see."

The other unicorns were fretting, stamping their feet, tails twitching. The younger ones, a couple of them only foals, were casting nervous glances behind them through the trees.

Midnight sighed as he saw Lottie watching. "For the last few days, we have tried not to keep in one place for very long. We've been watching, all the time, here in our own forest! All of us are anxious to . . . end this."

Lottie swallowed, and her throat felt tight. Pandora might want to get rid of Lottie and her father for ever, but Lottie had a feeling she wouldn't kill the unicorns. She would find a use for them, which would be worse.

Suddenly, one of the silver unicorns nearest to the trees whipped round and cantered towards them. "They're coming!" she hissed, tossing her head so that her heavy silver mane swung from side to side.

At once the herd moved in a silver-and-golden swirl, wheeling round so that they faced the oncoming threat.

Lottie realized that the unicorns had stopped running. Since she and her father had arrived, they were going to fight. She wrapped her arms tightly round Sofie, hoping that some of the little dog's unshakeable confidence would seep into her. She desperately didn't want to let the unicorns down, but she felt so fragile. Pandora was amazingly strong, and she had two others with her now. How could Lottie and her father hope to defeat her now that she had allies?

Lottie's father had moved in front of her, guarding her, but Lottie went to stand next to him instead, wrapping an arm around his waist. She didn't want to be behind him, safe, but not knowing what was happening.

You see, you said you were not ready, but you are. Sofie chuckled. *You want to fight her. I am going to bite her ankles,* she added happily.

I don't really want to, Lottie replied grimly. *I have to, that's all. What am I going to do, run away?*

You could.

No, I couldn't. Don't be silly. Sofie, look, I can see them!

All the unicorns had suddenly moved, lowering their heads so that their vicious horns faced outwards, ready to fight.

"Lottie, just be careful," her dad muttered, wrapping his fingers into hers as though he didn't want her to slip away from him. "Remember how clever she is at twisting things. Try to keep her out of your head."

Lottie nodded. She could see Pandora now, leading the other two, her black hood thrown back so that all her amazing white-blonde hair flowed down the back of her cloak. She was smiling widely.

The three of them stopped, about ten metres away, Pandora's two companions flanking her. They had hoods up around their faces and it was hard to see anything about them, except that they were both tall.

The unicorns were standing bravely between the two groups, but they were shifting and pawing the ground nervously. Clearly Pandora terrified them and only their loyalty to Lottie and her father was keeping them there. That, and Midnight. He was standing in the centre of the line, like a black stone statue of a horse. No one was going to move him.

But then, it didn't really matter; Lottie had seen Pandora in action before. It probably helped her if she could touch someone, but she certainly didn't need to.

Suddenly the two men in the black cloaks – Lottie was sure they were men, she didn't know why – took a step forward, and Lottie felt her father reel as though someone had hit him. The two unicorns closest to him closed in, holding him up, and one of them, a beautiful golden mare, gently lowered her head to press her horn into his hand. Lottie saw her father sigh and smile, opening his eyes. Lottie wished she'd asked him before about unicorn magic. Could unicorns break spells?

He had time to gasp, "Lottie, be careful!" but then he closed his eyes and started to weave his hands in complicated patterns, like some strange, slow dance. More unicorns drew in close, protecting him, a soft glow surrounding their gleaming horns as they worked their own magic to help him fight, adding to his spells.

Lottie let go of her dad and gulped in a panicky breath. She stared at Pandora, who had stepped a little closer. Lottie could see more than just her smile now; the eerie look of triumph in the enchantress's eyes was terrifying. Why did she think she had already won?

"Watch her," Sofie muttered, the fur on the back of her neck rising anxiously, and Midnight huffed in agreement, shaking his mane and pawing the ground. Lottie held Sofie in one arm and wound her fingers into Midnight's mane again. She sighed gratefully as she felt some of his determination seep under her fingernails.

Midnight was not going to let the herd be taken, and Lottie and Sofie were part of the herd now.

"You really think you can stop me?"

Pandora's voice was like the waterfall. Cool and beautiful and dangerous. The spells pouring and pouring, on and on, never stopping.

Lottie's fingers tightened in Midnight's mane so that it must have hurt, but he said nothing. His horn was aimed at Pandora's chest as she moved closer.

"I knew you would come. Dear, noble Tom, and it seems you've inherited his silly sentimental streak, Lottie. How terribly unlucky for you."

Lottie stared at her grimly. What she'd suspected was true. It was a set-up. A mad, elaborate trap. Pandora had wanted them to come, so she could have her grand revenge here, where she had defeated Lottie's father once before.

"Of course I wanted you to come, you silly little girl! Why else would I be in this awful place?" Pandora snorted with laughter. "I knew you and your idiot of a father couldn't resist an animal in distress, still less fifty of them."

"Lottie, I'm sorry!" Midnight's tail was swishing angrily. "I led you into a trap."

"No," Lottie shook her head. "I don't care if it's a trap, and Dad wouldn't either. He was desperate to help you, even before she turned up. Come on. There are so many of us, we're stronger than she is! Don't listen, don't let her frighten you!" She stared around at the unicorns. "This is your forest; we have to drive her out! She doesn't belong here!"

The unicorns pawed the ground, their long tails swishing, and paced forward, lowering their horns again.

But Pandora smiled. "Of course he was desperate to return. He was desperate to come here in the first place. That's why he left you. And now he's going to leave you again. You dragged him back just a little too soon, Lottie. He was almost there. . ."

"What do you mean?" Lottie asked, her heart starting to race.

"Do not listen to her!" Sofie snapped, but she was already too late. Lottie *had* listened.

"Almost a unicorn. That was what he wanted. He turned his back on his family once and he'll do it again. He was a unicorn in your dreams, wasn't he, Lottie?"

"Because you'd taken his memories away," Lottie said, but she could hear the hint of doubt in her own voice. "He came back!" she added strongly.

"You made him. He'd forgotten you. He didn't realize you could still drag him home. Oh, Lottie, how he must have cursed you." Pandora laughed, a light, tinkling chuckle.

"It isn't true. . ." Lottie whispered, but she was remembering her father's words: *the most amazing dream, the kind where you wake up and most desperately want it to be real.*

Was it what he had wanted after all? Were Lottie and her mother only second-best?

Lottie's fingers loosened themselves from Midnight's mane and she sat down on the grassy riverbank. She let go of Sofie and tried desperately to think back through all her dreams and visions of her father, through everything he'd said since he came back. She hardly noticed Pandora stalking closer, touching one of the unicorns, barely a colt. He was trembling, but he stood bravely, horn down, ready to fight. Until Pandora stared into his eyes and laid her hand upon his muzzle.

His knees gave way and he sank to the ground, his silvery horn now horribly discoloured.

Lottie didn't hear Pandora laughing as the other unicorns cried out in fear and dismay. But Sofie did.

Pandora came closer and her eyes darkened suddenly as she realized that she had caught Lottie — but she hadn't caught all of her.

Sofie planted a swift dog-kiss on Lottie's cheek and glared at Midnight, who obligingly lowered his shoulders so that she could leap on to his back.

Come on!

But we need to guard Lottie, Midnight protested.

We can't. Pandora is too strong for us. But Lottie can fight her, if we stop her thinking these stupid thoughts. This is the problem with Lottie. She thinks far too much. She should just have bitten the witch. It would have been better.

Pandora reached out a hand and swiped at Sofie, but Midnight jabbed his horn at her and she drew back, hissing. Sofie snarled.

Get me away from her! She cannot cross the water, can she? Take us into the river.

Midnight leapt. One long, amazing leap into the depths of the basin below the waterfall, and Sofie shook herself irritably as the silvery spray caught her. She looked back at Lottie, rocking herself quietly on the grass, and hissed. Then she closed her eyes. They were stupid not to have done this in the first place. Sofie raised her head and howled out loud, an eerie wail of a sound that made Pandora shiver, and Lottie's father and his two attackers break off their fight.

Lottie, wrapped in her loneliness, and feeling that no one wanted her, that she was useless, hardly heard.

At Grace's Pet Shop, Lottie's mother put her hands over her ears and Uncle Jack jumped up from the step he'd been sitting on, staring wildly around.

"That was Sofie! Something's wrong."

Lottie's mum ran her fingers over the wooden panelling, trying to find the little door, scratching and tearing with her nails. "It isn't here! Why isn't it coming back?" she gasped.

"We should have gone with her," Danny muttered, shaking his head to dislodge Sofie's shrieks. Ariadne put her arms around Lottie's mum, holding her back from the wall.

"Isobel, stop. You'll hurt yourself."

"I've only just got them back!" Lottie's mum pulled away, leaning against the wall. "I can't just wait and do nothing. Sofie was calling us, wasn't she?"

Uncle Jack frowned at her. "You heard Sofie, then?" he asked.

Lottie's mum glared at him. "Of course I heard her, she was howling like a fire engine. It was deafening."

"But she isn't anyway near here, Isobel; you heard her in your mind." He caught Lottie's mum's wrists, staring fiercely into her face. "Remember it. Where are they? Don't let the sound slip away, Isobel." He looked round at Ariadne and Danny. "Perhaps we can bring the door back, chase after them somehow if we all try together. Come on!"

Danny put his hand on top of Lottie's mother's, with Ariadne, but he looked up at his dad. "We don't need the door. Lottie never used it, the other times she went. The unicorns called her, like Sofie's calling us. We should just be able to answer the call."

Ariadne nodded. "He's right. Think of Lottie, and Sofie, and Tom. All think together."

The same black curly hair. The dark, round eyes, always looking surprised and excited. Hands that always seemed to be holding a creature; Lottie with her arms wrapped round Sofie, beaming. Tiny Lottie, chasing a butterfly, her father chasing after her laughing and swooping her up in the air like a butterfly herself.

Ariadne, Jack and Danny settled into the background, adding a memory here and there, nodding and smiling as Lottie's mother poured out a cascade of shining images, wrapped in her love for Lottie and her father. She was shaking, and Ariadne stood beside her, almost holding her up.

What would Lottie do in a forest? she whispered into Lottie's mum's thoughts, and Isobel laughed, the picture floating in her mind at once. She was watching Lottie running through the trees with Sofie galloping ahead of her, ears flapping madly as she bounced along.

Now Lottie had run on ahead, but Sofie was coming back. She was galloping towards them instead, the wisps of mist making her disappear every so often as she hurtled along. She was closer, almost close enough to touch now, her eyes huge and anxious.

"You came at last! Why are you so late? Hurry! Hurry!" And she leapt into Lottie's mother's arms, suddenly real. "Run!" she snapped, nipping furiously at her sleeve, and Lottie's mother stopped staring round her in amazement at the giant trees that had grown out of the stairs, and stumbled into a run. "Come on, she will hurt Lottie! Run!"

Danny was speeding ahead, making for the unicorns by the river, with Sep clinging tightly to his shoulder and muttering blood-curdling threats.

Lottie's father was still locked in a silent fight with one of the black-cloaked men, but the other had disappeared, though a torn black cloak was trailing in the water.

"Tom," Lottie's mother whispered, watching him strike at the air and the man opposite him reel away, shaking his head.

Uncle Jack grinned briefly. "He'll be fine. That one's no match for him. My guess is Pandora brought accomplices to keep Tom busy while she dealt with Lottie."

"But where is Lottie?" her mother demanded, looking around frantically. "I can't see her."

"She's there." Danny pointed at a huddled heap on the riverbank. His eyes were round with fear.

Pandora was sitting next to Lottie, her arms around her knees, smiling sweetly at them all as they crept closer.

"Is she . . . is she. . . ?" Lottie's mother stumbled over the words.

"No." Uncle Jack shook his head briskly.

"I can't make her hear me," Ariadne murmured, staring at the flash of red from Lottie's school cardigan. "It's almost as if she's shut everything out. Or shut down, somehow." She closed her eyes, trying to call to Lottie.

"Can't we get Pandora away from her?" Danny muttered. Sep was in his hands now, Danny cupping him tightly for comfort.

Lottie was curled up on the grass, trying to stay quiet and not move so that no one would notice her, ever. She had never felt so stupid. Of course her father would want to come back here, instead of staying in Netherbridge. Her mother had left her too.

But Sofie. . .

Sofie had loved her, hadn't she? Sofie had chosen to share her magic. Sofie pined for her when she was at school and raced to leap into her arms when she came back.

Lottie twitched a little as Pandora was distracted by the others and the spell lost its hold on her mind, just a little. Enough for Sofie to creep back in.

Sofie!

Don't move! Sofie's voice in her head was a shrill yap of warning. *Make her think that you are still bound.*

It was terribly hard to keep still once Sofie had said that. Lottie was suddenly desperate to scratch the end of her nose.

You are really very silly, Sofie told her reprovingly.

Where are you?

Behind you. I am lurking, Sofie added proudly. *That witch cannot see me. I have fetched your mother, and your uncle, and Danny and Ariadne. Even Tabitha. I did not invite her, but she came. Cats.*

Mum's here? Lottie's voice was panicky. *She mustn't be! What if Pandora does something to her?*

I think it is more likely that she will do something to Pandora. Your uncle is holding her back — look.

Lottie peered cautiously through the grass stems. Sofie was right. Her mother was struggling in Uncle Jack's arms, spitting insults at Pandora.

The enchantress had stood up. Even looking at her back, Lottie could tell that she was furious, now that she was confronted with her old rival again. The anger seemed to vibrate around her; the red dress she wore under her black cloak was a bright, humming scarlet now.

She is distracted, Sofie said thoughtfully.

Lottie caught her breath. She rolled her eyes painfully to try and see Sofie, behind her somewhere. She wanted to see her, to feel the comfort of her, to know Sofie loved her, after everything Pandora had said.

A delicious whiff of chocolate and vanilla came first, as Sofie wormed her way forward, burrowing through the grass stems to lie by Lottie's side and lick her cheek adoringly. *I thought for a very little moment that you were not coming back, Lottie mine.*

Sorry. She said awful things. She didn't dare say anything about you, though, Lottie realized. *I suppose she didn't even think of it. She doesn't understand about animals. She didn't know that only you could break me out of the spell.*

I love you too, Lottie, but this is not the time, Sofie told her briskly. But she shook her ears, as though she was happily embarrassed.

What are we going to do?

She is not expecting us to do anything. . . So we should attack her.

Lottie said nothing. She knew Sofie was right, but she felt as though any magic she'd ever had had drained away out of her, and she was a normal, boring little shell of a person. Pandora would stamp her underfoot, and she would be all gone.

She couldn't do it. Not even with Sofie; they simply weren't strong enough. Lottie blinked. The unicorns! Pandora's dreadful attack on the colt had left them huddled together, lost and frightened. But if Lottie could get them to fight with her again. . .

I will help.

Lottie dug her fingernails into the earth to stop herself squawking in surprise. An image of Midnight, waiting half-hidden behind the waterfall, flashed into her mind.

I am ready. Sofie is right. The enchantress is distracted, angry at your mother. We should attack now.

Lottie swallowed. *Sofie, I know you're going to hate me, but I don't want to hurt her. I know it's probably a mistake, like it was before, but I just can't.*

Sofie sniffed out loud. *I know*, she told Lottie, letting Midnight hear too. *It is a mistake, perhaps, but it is also you. We cannot change you.*

But if we just chase her away again — even if we could do that — then it won't be finished. Lottie sighed. *I just want it to stop.*

Midnight replied, *There is a way. She would not be hurt. She might even be happier than she is now. You have to get her into the water, to me, but it will be hard. She knows she can't touch it. You must make her so angry that she will do it anyway.*

Lottie took a deep breath and began to fish delicately for Pandora's thoughts. They were not hard to find; her seething anger was bubbling out of her everywhere. Lottie slid a picture of what Pandora would hate most of all into the enchantress's mind. Lottie herself, with her parents behind her, their arms around each other, all smiling. Sofie was in Lottie's arms and the other animals from the shop were there too — Horace, Fred, Giles. Even sweet and silly Barney was sitting on her mother's shoulder.

Pandora screamed. She seemed to think it was Lottie's mother who had created the vision, and she leapt at the spell-picture as though she wanted to claw at Isobel's face.

But the family in front of Pandora only laughed and turned away, walking out across the water and leaving her behind. Always leaving her behind.

Furious, Pandora strode after them, not seeing that she was walking into the water. And that behind her was a tide of unicorns, guiding her further into the rushing river.

Lottie's spell-family disappeared into the sparkling spray of the waterfall, breaking apart into a cloud of shimmering water-droplets. Lottie could see Midnight's reflection through the water as she stood on the bank, holding Sofie. She hoped she'd done enough and his plan would work.

It took only a few moments for Pandora to understand what she had done and she cried out in horror, turning back to make for the bank.

But there was nowhere to go. The unicorns were all around her now, pressing her back into the waterfall, so that her streaming white-blonde hair began to darken in the water, then the frothing whiteness closed over her entirely.

And then the black unicorn appeared, walking out from under the falls alone, stepping proudly through the river, his mane floating around him. Lottie stared at him in horror, wondering what he had done with Pandora, but he only whinnied, as though he was laughing. "Watch, Lottie," Midnight told her, nudging her gently.

Out of the waterfall came a shimmering shape, as a golden-white unicorn stepped slowly through the torrent, picking her way delicately and shaking her glittering white mane.

"You turned her into a unicorn!" Lottie murmured, and Sofie sneezed in amazement.

"I didn't know you could do that!"

Midnight nuzzled her again. "It can be done. When it needs to be so. Or if someone wants it more than anything. We could have changed your father, Lottie, if he had wanted. But he wanted something else more, even though he didn't know what it was."

Lottie rested her cheek against his smooth nose gratefully.

"Is she still – her?" she asked, watching Pandora swimming and scrambling out on to the bank, lovingly surrounded by the rest of the herd.

Midnight nudged Lottie with his horn, gently motioning her to climb on his back. When she was sitting side-saddle, he swam after the white unicorn. "She is. But she won't remember. And she will be happier like this. I promise you, Lottie."

They climbed out on to the other bank, and Lottie half-jumped, half-fell off Midnight's back and into her mother's arms, wrapping herself so tightly that her mum laughed.

"I can't believe you're here." Lottie smiled. "This is a magic place, and you're here."

"Lottie, you did it." Her father walked towards them, his arm around the neck of the silvery colt that Pandora had attacked. The young unicorn looked dazed, and seemed to be leaning against Lottie's dad as though his legs were still shaky, but he was alive.

Lottie's mum gazed at him, smiling. "She did, Tom. But you were there with her. You and Jack, and Danny and Ariadne and Sofie. Even me. We did it. All of us." Then she gasped. "Lottie, turn round, you can't miss this."

Lottie turned, her mother's arms still crossed around her, and caught her breath as the unicorns galloped away, the crystal-white mare swallowed into the middle of the herd. Midnight blew lovingly into Lottie's ear, and thundered after them, disappearing once again in between the dark trees.

Up on Netherbridge Hill, wrapped in winter coats and sharing Ruby's enormous stripy knitted scarf, Lottie and Ruby stared out across the sweet-smelling turf. It was five o'clock on the evening of Lottie's eleventh birthday. Two weeks had passed since Lottie had dragged her family into the forest, and she had heard nothing from the unicorns since that night. But she was sure something was about to happen.

"Shouldn't we get back?" Ruby suggested, her teeth chattering slightly. "Your mum's made you a cake. I could really do with some cake, Lottie; I'm frozen."

"Now!" Sofie yapped excitedly.

"I knew it!" Lottie laughed. "I knew they would. Ruby, watch!"

Streaming down the side of the valley came a herd of unicorns, silver and white and gold. And just one black one. They pounded past, making the girls shiver with their thundering hooves, and Lottie and Ruby laughed out loud in delight.

They galloped past and away, and Ruby whispered, "Lottie, were they real?"

Lottie smiled. "Maybe not here. But somewhere they were."

Although Sofie drinks enormous amounts of coffee and gobbles chocolate, this is only because she is a magical dog. Chocolate can be very dangerous for dogs, so please don't feed your dogs chocolate, or anything that isn't their normal food. Even if you suspect they're magical inside!

–HW

Ready for more

adventures with Lottie?

Here's a sneak peek of

Animal Magic

Mousemagic

HOLLY WEBB

Chapter 1

Lottie hurried through Netherbridge with Ruby. Sofie, Lottie's dog, waltzed around their feet, her long dachshund ears blowing in the cold November wind. The girls had been up on Netherbridge Hill, and they were late going home – Lottie's mum was cooking her a special birthday dinner, but Lottie was sure that she'd understand. She wished her mum could have been up on the hill with them, to see the herd of unicorns galloping past.

"Ugh, it's so dark!" Ruby moaned as they scuttled down the street to the pet shop. "Wintry."

Lottie shivered. "If it had been this cold last weekend, we wouldn't have needed to go to Linford for my skating party. We could have just skated on the river."

Just before they reached the shop, Ruby pulled Lottie's sleeve. "Listen, I just want to say thank you, Lottie. Seeing the unicorns like that, thundering down the hill. I think it was the best thing I've ever seen. They were so beautiful."

Lottie smiled, and gave Ruby a quick hug. "They're amazing, aren't they? I think that might be the best birthday present ever."

Lottie had woken that morning with the fleeting wisps of a dream, the horsey voice of Midnight, the black unicorn, laughing in her ear and telling her *Happy birthday*. She knew she had to go to Netherbridge Hill – it had been hard to live through a whole day at school first.

Now, she flung the door of the pet shop open, sighing delightedly as the warm, rather stuffy, slightly mouse-smelling, air wafted round her. Lottie leant against the glass door, smiling.

Every so often, when she walked into the shop, she would get a sudden rush of astonishment that she really lived here. She was so lucky.

It was hardly surprising that she was happy. Lottie had adored Grace's Pet Shop when it only contained her uncle Jack and her cousin Danny. She had always loved animals, and living in a pet shop was like a dream come true, even if at first her uncle and Danny had been a bit weird and secretive.

It hadn't taken her that long to find out why. Grace's was no ordinary pet shop. All the animals could talk – in fact, several of them found it hard to stop. Uncle Jack had an amazing magic with animals, a magic that ran in the family, and wonderfully, Lottie had it too.

But now the shop seemed even more precious and special. Her father was there, for a start, looking just like a more tanned version of Uncle Jack. Even more brilliantly, Lottie's mother was in the kitchen, making Lottie's favourite tea, shepherd's pie. To most people, that wouldn't sound all that strange, Lottie thought to herself — except that for years everyone had thought her dad was dead. And until just a few weeks before, her mum had been living and working in Paris. It was why Lottie had been dumped at the shop back at the beginning of the summer — that was how she'd thought of it then. Now it was the best thing that had ever happened to her.

Her mum was mashing potatoes and humming to herself, but she glanced up as Lottie and Ruby came into the kitchen, and the look on her face made Lottie feel like singing — loudly. There was a smear of mashed potato down her mum's cheek and her hair was falling out of its ponytail, and she was beaming. Lottie had never seen her look prettier. Her dad was sitting at the table, pretending to look at a catalogue for a pet food company, but actually watching her mum. They weren't back together as a couple — they had been apart for so long, eight whole years, and were still getting to know each other again – but Lottie was hoping.

"Did you see them?" Lottie's mum asked, rubbing absent-mindedly at the potato streak, her eyes searching Lottie's face eagerly.

Lottie nodded slowly. She felt almost as though she were dreaming. Her mother, her own mother, the person who couldn't stand animals, and laughed at anything even slightly mysterious, let alone magical, was asking if she'd seen a herd of unicorns.

The unicorns came from a lost forest in the foothills of the Himalayas. Her dad had lived with them, trapped without his memory, for all that time he had been missing. He had almost been transformed into a unicorn, and only Lottie's growing magic had brought him home, the magic fizzing in her blood calling to his. Lottie had thought the strange encounters she'd had with a silver unicorn were only dreams. She hadn't known she was gradually breaking the spell that had been put on her own father.

It was the kind of story her sensible mother would never have believed. Lottie hadn't known it, but her mum's disbelieving attitude to magic had been partly down to her dad's old girlfriend. Pandora had never got over breaking up with Lottie's dad. She had been crazily, murderously jealous, and she'd been the one who sent Lottie's dad off to get lost in the unicorns' forest. She'd also poisoned Lottie's mum's mind to magic. But Pandora was gone now – banished to the rainforest herself.

A pair of soft grey ears appeared over the edge of the table, and then, slowly, a greyish-pink nose and a pair of dark, solemn eyes. Barney the rabbit had come to investigate what his favourite person was doing.

"Hello, Barney darling," Lottie's mum stroked the back of her arm across his ears. Barney had helped to turn her back into an animal person, and she adored him, but she would never have dreamed of stroking an animal with her hand while she was in the middle of cooking. Lottie sort of understood this, and she could see why it was a good idea, but she and Uncle Jack still caught each other's eye. Uncle Jack usually cooked with an owl on one shoulder and quite possibly a mouse or two in his hair. The owl, Horace, was actually a phoenix in disguise, but Lottie was pretty sure phoenixes weren't particularly hygienic either.

"More butter, if you please." Sofie popped up on the other side of the table and stared critically at the pan of mashed potato. "It looks dry to me."

Lottie's mum raised one eyebrow, but then she shrugged, and stirred the potato thoughtfully. "Perhaps a little," she conceded.

Sofie nodded as she stirred it in, and sniffed the buttery steam with her eyes closed. "*Magnifique.*" Then she snapped her eyes open again and glared at Lottie's mum. "Of course, it is not French cuisine," she pointed out sternly.

"Of course not." Lottie's mum passed a spoonful of potato quite close to Sofie's nose. "Does that mean you don't want any?"

"When in Rome. . ." Sofie said in a long-suffering voice. "I am not one to complain. Ever."

"It smells fantastic," Lottie murmured, giving her mum a quick one-arm hug so as not to get in the way of the dinner. "Will it be long? It was freezing out on the hill and I'm so hungry."

"Me too," Ruby added. "It looks great."

"Did they look all right, the unicorns?" Lottie's dad asked, rather wistfully. "Was it the whole herd?"

"I think so." Lottie half-closed her eyes, remembering and trying to count. "Definitely fifty at least. They came galloping across the ridge. It was amazing. Ruby nearly fell over, it was so exciting."

"I've never seen anything like that." Ruby sat down at the table, her chin in her hands, smiling.

"There." Lottie's mum finished spooning the mash over the pie, and slid it into the oven. "That should be ready before we know it."

"Where's Danny?" Lottie asked. "Is he upstairs?"

Uncle Jack nodded. "In his room."

"Are you two planning on changing for this special birthday dinner?" Lottie's mum asked, her voice very bright. Lottie took the hint. Uncle Jack was looking gloomy enough as it was. It looked like Danny had done something wrong. Probably he'd been rude to Lottie's mum again; he seemed to be doing that a lot at the moment.

Ever since she and Lottie's dad had both been back at the shop, Danny had been very moody. Lottie hated it. Danny's mum had died a few years ago, and it had been something that tied him and Lottie together – only having one parent. Now Lottie had a whole perfect family, and Danny was furiously, meanly jealous.

Ruby had brought some things to change into, so they headed upstairs, Sofie galloping in front of them. She had a selection of glittery collars, and clearly she wanted to dress up too.

"This is great, having a special family party," Ruby told Lottie.

Lottie grinned. "I know. Mum and me always had a special meal on my birthday, but it was just the two of us. This year it's huge. And I've already had my proper party with you and people from school last weekend." She ran a brush through her black curly hair, tugging it thoughtfully. "I feel spoilt."

Sofie pushed in front of Ruby to see herself in the mirror. "Hmm. The purple crystals, I think. Lottie, fasten me." She held out her long neck gracefully. *"Merci, ma petite.* Are we ready?" She gazed round at Ruby and Lottie, rather like a bossy little headmistress, and trotted out of the room, with the girls trooping after her.

Uncle Jack was at the bottom of the stairs, having words with Danny. ". . .Lottie's birthday! Just behave yourself!" He shut up quickly when he heard Sofie's claws clattering on the wooden treads, and shooed Danny into the kitchen.

"Still causing trouble, then?" Ruby whispered. She usually got on well with Danny – they'd been at the same school until this year, when he'd gone off to secondary school.

"All the time," Lottie muttered. "But I can see why, I guess." She sighed. She hoped Danny got used to the way things were soon. She didn't think she could bear it if her mum or dad ended up leaving again.

"She's coming, she's coming!" A whisper ran round the cages in the shop as Lottie and Ruby reached the bottom of the stairs. A moving, mottled carpet of mice rushed in front of them to reach the kitchen first, and a chorus of different voices called, "Happy birthday, Lottie!"

The mice were lined up all along the shelves of the dresser, dancing and squeaking with excitement. Lottie's favourite pink mouse, Fred, had made himself a matching pink party hat, a dashing, pointed creation, which threatened to fall off every time he moved.

"He looks ridiculous," Sofie muttered. She found Fred deeply irritating, and would not admit that it was because she was jealous. She was Lottie's familiar, her special one, but she could never quite believe that Lottie loved her best.

Lottie looked round the kitchen hopefully, wondering where her presents were. She had agreed to have them after tea, so that there wasn't a rush before school, but now the waiting was starting to get to her.

They must be all hidden away somewhere, the cake too, Lottie thought. At least, she hoped so. Maybe everyone thought eleven was too old for proper presents.

But the table looked beautiful, with loads of tiny candles glittering all over it, and all her family packed around. It was a squash to fit everyone in. Ariadne – Uncle Jack's girlfriend, who taught Lottie magic – had arrived and was sitting next to Uncle Jack. Tabitha, her cat familiar, was balanced on her shoulder, blinking slowly at the mice, who were trying very hard to ignore her. They *knew* that Tabitha would never chase them here, but their instincts were still telling them that she wanted *them* for dinner, not shepherd's pie.

"Is it time for presents yet?" Fred asked hopefully, as soon as Lottie had taken a bite of pie. "You said when you'd eaten!" he complained, as Uncle Jack shook his head. "Honestly, I do wish you'd all hurry up."

Lottie smiled in secret relief. So there were going to be presents. She'd known it really, but just for a moment. . . She felt almost as impatient as Fred.

"Now?" Fred squeaked. He'd skittered up the tablecloth as Lottie's mum was clearing the plates, and was now sitting next to a small tea light holder by Lottie, warming his paws and exchanging dirty looks with Sofie.

"Cake first." Uncle Jack got up to turn the lights off, so that only the candles lit the room. Hundreds of tiny, eager eyes glittered in the flickering light.

"Oh. . ." Lottie breathed, as her mother walked in from the shop – where on earth had they hidden the cake so that no one nibbled it? She smiled to herself. Perhaps they'd set Horace to guard it. In his owl shape, he was most of the mice's worst nightmare.

It was huge. Pink and white icing, with eleven tall pink candles. Lottie's mum had always made fabulous birthday cakes, but this one was so grown-up.

"Happy birthday dear Lottie, happy birthday to you. . .!" Growls and squeaks joined together, and everyone finished at a different time, but Lottie didn't mind. The happiness rippled in the air. The mice, especially, seemed to be in a state of nervous excitement that made Lottie's heart race like theirs were. There was a secret, something terribly exciting. She could feel it inside her.

Lottie's dad had put an armful of parcels in front of her while her mum was cutting up the cake, and now he grinned at her. "I'd hurry up, before Fred has a heart attack."

"I am perfectly all right, thank you!" Fred declared, standing up and sticking out his chest. But then he spoilt the effect by twisting his tail between his tiny paws, and adding, "But do please hurry, Lottie! We want to give you our present!" Then he sat down very quickly, with a nervous giggle.

Lottie stared at the presents, wondering which to open first. In the end she closed her eyes, and reached. A small silver-wrapped parcel. No ribbon. From her dad. She smiled at him, and undid the tape. Inside was a little velvet bag, and Lottie opened it curiously. Into her hand fell a delicate coil of silver chain, with a silver unicorn dangling from it. The pendant was only tiny, but as Lottie stared at it, she could see every hair. She could feel its heart beating under her fingers, and if she closed her eyes, she could smell the rich, earthy steam of the rainforest.

"Midnight's hair is inside it," her father explained. "The one we used to get back to the rainforest. I thought you'd like it – I don't know if we'll ever go back. . ."

"I love it. Thank you. . ." She hugged him, and he fastened it carefully round her neck.

"Go on! Go on!" Fred was dancing about again.

Lottie's mum had given her a bracelet that matched the unicorn necklace (which was good, Lottie noted at the back of her mind, as it meant that her mum and dad had talked about presents together). Ruby's present was a cool velvet scarf, purple with silvery stripes.

Uncle Jack had given her a book on scorpions, which Lottie rather thought he'd wanted for himself, and Ariadne's present was a big, purple-covered book, embossed on the front cover with SPELLS. But it turned out to be empty.

"You have to write the spells in, Lottie, when you make them up," Ariadne told her, chuckling at her confused face. "That will be the next stage of your training— refining and perfecting your spells, and writing them down."

Sofie nudged a small package towards her. She was pretending not to care what Lottie thought, gulping at her cake as Lottie undid it, but she was glaring sharply sideways. It had no tape or ribbon, which made Lottie think that Sofie had wrapped it herself, which must have been almost impossible with paws. "Oh, Sofie," she murmured, as she pulled it out. A tiny gold-framed painting of a dachshund. It wasn't quite Sofie – the nose was longer – but it was very like her.

"My grandmother." Sofie ducked her nose proudly as Lottie kissed her head. "It is old. Take care, yes?"

"Of course I will."

Danny made a dismissive sort of snorting noise, and Lottie looked up in surprise. Sofie leaned further forward over the table, and hissed, "You have something to say, Daniel, huh?"

"Do you have a present for Lottie, Danny?" Uncle Jack asked hurriedly, trying to smooth things over.

"No," Danny snapped. "What else does she need? She's got everything, hasn't she?" He scraped his chair back with a nerve-jarring screech, grabbed Septimus, his black rat, and ran off upstairs, banging the kitchen door behind him.

Everyone sat staring at each other dumbly, until Fred squeaked. "More presents!"

"Yes, yes! Now us, now us!" The mice chittered and giggled, and Fred scurried off the table to be surrounded by a crowd of overexcited mice on the front of the dresser.

"Hurry up!" Lottie could hear him hissing. "No, not that tight, I'll faint! There!" and the mice drew back, letting Fred stand in front of them all, blushing a darker pink than usual.

He was wearing a large purple satin ribbon tied in a bow around his middle, and his whiskers were drooping with bashfulness.

"This is our present," he gabbled. "Me."

Join Lottie in all of her

adventures.

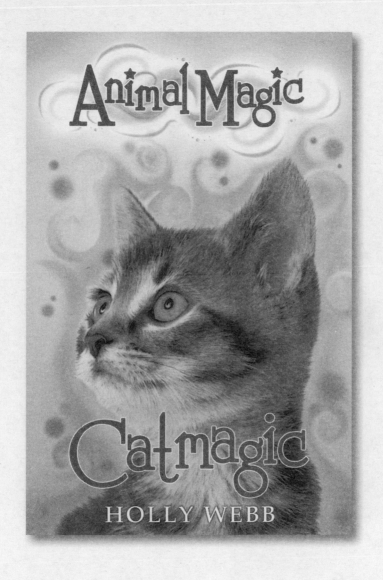

Animal Magic

Catmagic

HOLLY WEBB

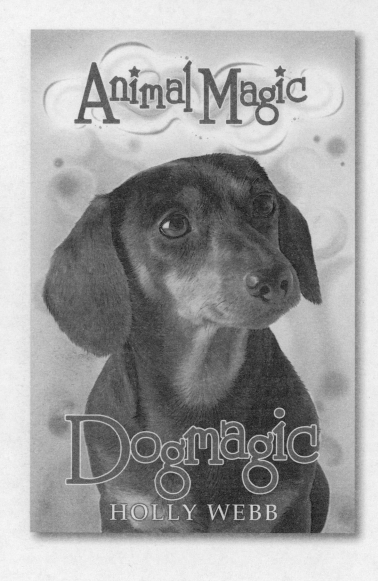

Animal Magic

Dogmagic

HOLLY WEBB

Animal Magic

Hamstermagic

HOLLY WEBB

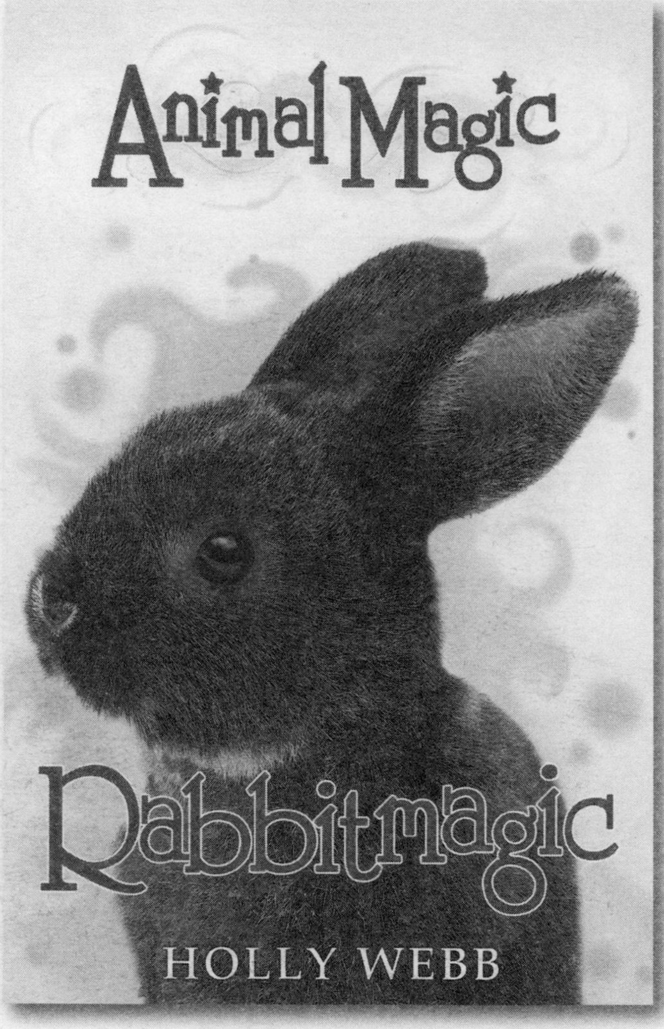
Animal Magic
Rabbitmagic
HOLLY WEBB

Enter the magical world of

the ordinary girl in an
extraordinary family...

HOLLY WEBB

EMILY
FEATHER
and the Enchanted Door

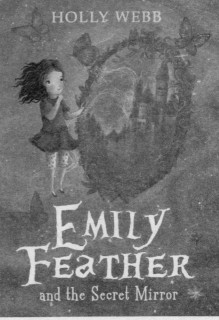

HOLLY WEBB

EMILY
FEATHER
and the Secret Mirror

Holly has always loved animals. As a child, she had two dogs, a cat, and at one point, nine gerbils (an accident). Holly's other love is books. Holly now lives in Reading with her husband, three sons and a very spoilt cat.